One Voice, Please

Please

Favorite Read-Aloud Stories

Sam McBratney

illustrated by
Russell Ayto

CANDLEWICK PRESS
CAMBRIDGE, MASSACHUSETTS

Text copyright © 2005 by Sam McBratney
Illustrations copyright © 2005 by Russell Ayto

First U.S. edition 2008

Library of Congress Cataloging-in-Publication Data is available.

Library of Congress Catalog Card Number pending

ISBN 978-0-7636-3479-7

2 4 6 8 10 9 7 5 3

Printed in the United States of America

This book was typeset in Horley Old Style.

Candlewick Press
2067 Massachusetts Avenue
Cambridge, Massachusetts 02140

visit us at www.candlewick.com

CONTENTS

INTRODUCTION

YOUR COLLECTOR OF STORIES remembers stopping to eat in southern Ireland years ago.

The place was a family pub, full of people relaxing around a turf fire and—so it seemed—all talking at once. Suddenly the landlord called out, "One voice, please. One voice only, please."

A hush fell over the company as a small man sitting in the chimney corner cleared his throat. He wore a battered hat and had huge red ears. And then, fixing his eyes on a thatch peg in the roof, he began to tell a story.

That was the moment when this collection began. I've been collecting stories that have been told down the ages ever since. These are some of my favorites. You and I are present in these tales of truth and trickery.

So, hush: one voice only, please. . . .

People are full of rage nowadays; you must have seen this for yourself. But is there anything new about road rage and supermarket cart rage? Not a bit; rage is as old as the human race.

DINNER OUTSIDE

A SERVANT had a short-tempered master, who came down to Sunday dinner in a bad mood.

"The soup is too hot!" he raged, and thumped the table.

Well, if the soup hadn't been too hot, it would have been too cold, for no soup could have pleased him that day. He would have picked a fight with the perfect bowl of soup. Lifting the dish, he pitched it, soup and all, out of the open window into the yard below.

The good servant who had brought the soup did not hesitate for a moment. He threw the meat he was bringing to the table straight out of the window. Then the bread. And after the bread went the jug of wine. As a matter of fact, he threw the tablecloth and every item on it out of the window and into the yard, too. There

was a terrible tinkling of falling cutlery and breaking glass

"What the devil do you think you're doing?" cried the master, rising to his feet.

The good servant looked at him out of marvelously innocent eyes. "Have I misunderstood your intentions? Pardon me, Master, but when I saw the soup leave the room, I thought you wanted to eat outside today. After all, the weather is warm, the sky is blue . . . and, behold, the bees are buzzing around the apple blossom!"

It was a fine lesson in how to deal with bad manners. One hopes that the master had the character to learn from it, and that the soup never flew out of the window again.

**Money gives everybody trouble
at one time or another.**

WITNESSES

THERE WAS once a man—neither the first nor the last—who had a problem with a loan. This is how he explained the problem to his friends at the inn.

"I lent ten silver crowns to a cousin of mine, who shows no sign of paying them back. And now I need the money. He just laughs when I ask him, and I'm beginning to wonder if I'll ever see my ten crowns again. If only I had witnesses! But I gave him the money in private, so I can't prove it. The fellow could deny everything."

His friends, all too familiar with the horrors of borrowing and lending money, made sympathetic noises.

Then the innkeeper spoke. "If it's a witness you're after, I can help you there."

"How?"

"Ask your cousin to come here tomorrow night. Remind him quietly in front of us all that he still owes you a hundred silver crowns."

"But I only lent him ten!"

"Aye, that's what he'll say, too," said the innkeeper. "And you shall have your witnesses."

You can work wonders when you're
highly motivated. Ask Master Hound.

THE RUNNING HARE

ONE MORNING in March, a dog went after a hare in
the meadow. It was a mighty chase, in and out of the
rushes and the bushes. At the last moment, the hare
gave a jump and a twist, and escaped into open country.

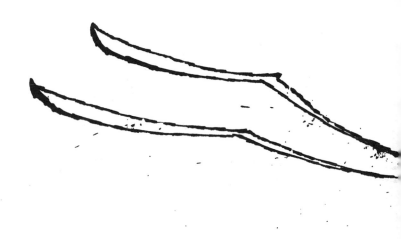

An old fellow had been watching all of this through a gap in the hedge.

He said, "Well, Master Hound, I see that Hare had the beating of you this morning."

"Don't pretend to be surprised," replied the dog, still panting after his exertions. "I was running for my lunch, but the hare . . . he was running for his life."

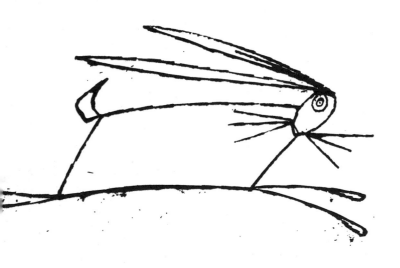

DAYDREAMING

ONCE THERE WAS a potter who surpassed himself by making a lovely pot. This new pot had a tall, elegant shape, with a glaze as blue as cornflowers and fancy bits curling around the neck. All in all, it was a work of art. Off he went to the market, carrying the pot in his arms and determined to sell it for nothing less than a shilling.

The potter paused to rest on a bridge and began to think how nice it would be if he were to get more than a shilling for his pot. *This might be my lucky day,* he said to himself. *A rich lady passing by might stop her carriage and buy my pot for a silver crown!*

Then he began to think what he could do with a whole silver crown. He could buy enough clay to make ten pots and have ten more silver crowns—and then he could buy one of those little boats anchored along the river. After a few years of being a potter and a fisherman, he could almost certainly afford a bigger boat—in fact, a ship. Then he would come sailing home from the east with the hold full of silks and spices, and the beautiful daughter of a rich merchant would fall in love with him. . . .

This mighty chain of events seemed so real to the potter on the bridge that he looked to see whether a rich lady in a carriage might be passing this way. Alas, it mattered not, for as he turned, he knocked the pot off the bridge. Down it fell, spinning over and over, until it smashed on the rocks below.

There was nothing to do but go home. *So much for daydreaming,* thought the potter. *Next time I'll take my pot straight to the market, and I'll sell it to the first soul who offers me a shilling.*

GENTLE PERSUASION

THE WIND met the Sun one day and boasted about how strong he was.

"I'm the strongest thing there is in the world," said the Wind. "Look how I can uproot trees and drive the raging ocean. I hope you'll agree with me, Sun, that there's nothing as powerful as I am—not even you." And, as if to prove his point, he blew a few clouds across the face of the Sun.

"There are many ways of being powerful," replied the Sun, quickly drying up the clouds.

"But look at the names people have for me. You are only the Sun, but me, I am the cyclone, the storm, the tempest, the hurricane, and the gale—the one they truly fear!"

On the earth below, there happened to be a peasant going to work along a country lane. Over his clothes he wore a rough and loosely fitting blanket, and the Wind said, "Let's put our power to the test, and see which of us can make the man take off his blanket."

"Whatever pleases you," said the Sun. "You may go first, if you like."

So the Wind began to blow. There were times when the man in the country lane seemed likely to be blown right off his feet; indeed, the little leather pouch that held his lunch was snatched from his hand and flung

five fields away. But he wrapped his blanket around him. The more it flapped in the sudden storm, the tighter he clutched it, and then, because the blanket had no buttons, he produced a bale of twine from a pocket and tied it twice around his middle. The Wind had to accept that he could not part the man from his blanket.

Now it was the turn of the Sun. She rose in the sky and shone so brightly that before long the man loosened the twine around his middle. Even so, he began to sweat. After kneeling by the river to have a drink, he puffed out his cheeks, wiped his brow, then removed the blanket completely. The Wind had to admit that power is not the same as brute force and may be used gently on some occasions.

There's many a crafty thief in this world, as a
woodcutter discovered one market day.

THE SECOND SHOE

IT WAS the harvest market, one of the grand occasions
of the year. Local farmers came to sell their fruits and
vegetables. Monks and nuns brought their abbey wines,
and from far away came merchants with silk and spices
to sell, and pet monkeys, mother-of-pearl, and feathers
of flamingos. There were dancing bears and singing
minstrels to coax the pennies from your pocket, but the
woodcutter didn't have to spend a thing on entertainment—it was enough to stare at a heap of crabs for
sale or to watch the crowd howl with fury when they
suspected a pickpocket.

Of all the things the woodcutter saw at the market,
he fancied most a lovely side of ham, which he bought
to take home for his family. It would keep the five of
them well provided with meat for many a day. Lifting
the ham onto his shoulder—for a woodcutter has no

fear of a heavy load—he set off for home along the quiet road.

The woodcutter had no idea that a thief was watching him from the bushes.

This thief was also a great lover of ham and could easily imagine thin slices of it melting away in his mouth. Then he imagined the slices cut thickly, needing to be chewed and then washed down with beer until nothing remained but the tangy taste of the salt. *I have to have that ham,* thought the thief.

But how to get it was the problem! The most obvious thing would be to wallop the woodcutter with a stick, but he was a hefty-looking sort, and the thief could see that he might end up getting walloped himself. No, if he was to get his hands on that ham, he had to do it by thinking. . . .

Presently the woodcutter came to where the road passed through the shade of some trees. He had just swung the weight of his ham from one shoulder to the other when he saw a shoe lying on the ground: a single shoe. It seemed to be a reasonably good shoe, but in truth he paid little attention to it, for one shoe on its own is not much use when you have two feet, and, anyway, he didn't want the bother of putting down and lifting up the side of ham. So he left the shoe lying where it was.

But when he went around two more bends in the road, there he saw another shoe. This time he stopped for a closer look. The shoe had seen better days, no doubt, but was still sound enough for all that. And, more to the point, it looked like a match for the one back up the road. "Sure I might as well have these shoes as the next man," said the woodcutter. "If they don't fit me, they'll fit somebody in the family." So he set down the ham and went back for the first shoe.

The woodcutter couldn't find the other shoe—it seemed to have just disappeared. When he came back, he discovered that the second shoe had disappeared, too. And so had his lovely side of ham.

One story about shoes brings to mind another.
Your Collector of Stories recalls Mamoud the
Grumbler, to whom life never seemed fair.

IN SOMEONE ELSE'S SHOES

EACH FRIDAY it is the duty of Muslims to go to the mosque and join with others in worship. The men take off their shoes and leave them outside to show respect for the holy place of Allah.

Now it happened one Friday that Mamoud had no shoes to wear. His old shoes were ready to fall apart, and he hadn't yet saved up enough money for new ones. The only thing he could do was go in bare feet and hope that no one would notice that he had no shoes to leave outside.

"What a miserable cur I am," he grumbled on the way to the mosque. "I can't even afford to look after my feet!" And, of course, once he got there and saw everyone else's shoes sitting on the stone steps, he felt worse. There were slippers as thin as carpet, simple shoes

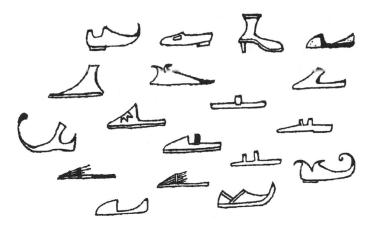

made from rushes, fancy shoes of leather, some with straps and some without, low heels, high heels, pointy-toes, and no-toes. "Why is everyone else so lucky?" moaned Mamoud. "Why am I the only one without a proper pair of shoes?"

Into the mosque he went, feeling so sorry for himself that he could hardly join in the prayers. But then, he suddenly found himself wondering about the person in front of him, for Mamoud could not see his feet. They appeared to be hidden under the man's loose clothing. It came as quite a shock to Mamoud when he realized that the truth was very different: the man in front of him had no feet.

As he walked home from the mosque that Friday, Mamoud's thoughts were not about himself. He was far too ashamed for that. To moan so bitterly about having no shoes! To complain about being poor when there were people so much worse off than he was! Perhaps for the first time in his life, Mamoud realized all the good things about himself that he had taken for granted and for which he had never expressed the slightest thanks.

There is a saying that it does you good to walk a mile in another person's shoes. It certainly worked for Mamoud.

There are many stories to be told about the Wise Men of Gotham, but I will only tell you about the time they (almost) counted up to twelve.

LOST WHILE FISHING

ONE DAY, twelve Wise Men of Gotham went fishing. They agreed to catch one fish each—and only one fish each—so as to leave enough in the river for another day.

Well, eventually they got started. One Wise Man of Gotham hooked another Wise Man of Gotham by the trousers and pulled him off his feet. Yet another Wise Man of Gotham hooked himself by the trousers and pulled himself off his feet. Two of them fell into the river. At least six ran away from a floating log, all screaming, "Crocodile!" And then the first one to catch a fish got so excited that he danced on all the packed lunches and squashed them.

Strange to tell, they managed to catch one fish each. They laid them out on the riverbank to count them, and, sure enough, there were twelve fish.

"Maybe we should count ourselves," suggested one of the Wise Men. "We've been in and out of the water so much that one of us might have drowned."

"Could be," agreed another.

"Let's count, then," said a third.

Each Wise Man of Gotham counted the group, but since each one forgot to count himself, the total never got past eleven. Panic set in.

"One's lost!"

"Who's missing?"

"One of us has drowned!"

Off they ran to search among the bushes and the rushes, to poke into the duckweed and the reeds. But of course they had to give up, for there was no one missing at all. A horseman riding by, seeing their miserable faces, asked them what was the matter.

"Well may you ask, friend. As you see, we have twelve fish, but only eleven people. One of our party is missing, and he is nowhere to be found. He must have drowned, we think."

The horseman looked carefully at the Wise Men of Gotham standing before him. "If I find your missing companion, will you give me your fish?"

"Aye, sir! And all the money in our pockets."

"Then there goes Number One!" cried the horseman, tapping the first Wise Man of Gotham on the shoulder with his riding whip. "Go and pick up a fish."

He did so.

"Number Two. Pick up a fish!"

Number Two picked up a fish—and Number Three. And Number Four. And thus in sequence he numbered them, until the twelve men were matched with twelve fish.

"Ah, sir, bless you for riding by," said the Wise Men of Gotham, pressing him to accept all of their fish and all of their money.

Then they went home. On the way, a Wise Man of Gotham said out loud: "I wonder which one of us was the fool who got lost?"

No one answered. *Aha,* thought each Wise Man of Gotham, *the fellow is ashamed of himself and won't admit a thing!*

This is the story of a king whose math was not much better than the Wise Men of Gotham.

MANY LITTLES MAKE A LOT

ONCE THERE WAS a king who played games of dice with the noblemen of his court. And when he lost—which he often did—he paid off his debts by giving away parts of his kingdom: a timber wood, perhaps, or a copper mine, or a salmon river far away. The king

insisted that he never lost very much, but one of his most honest advisers thought otherwise. The man's name was Pasha, and he often warned the king about gambling.

"But I only lose a little now and then, Pasha."

"Many littles make a lot," Pasha would say, frowning when the dice appeared once again.

To take the king's mind off throwing dice, Pasha invented the game of chess. It was a game between two armies played on a board of sixty-four squares, and in no time the king fell under its spell. Working out moves to make on the chessboard was a lot more interesting than trying to throw double sixes.

"Pasha," said the king, "you must have a reward for inventing this game. Ask me for anything—within reason, of course. You shall have it."

"It isn't necessary, Sire."

"Yes it is! Come on, your reward."

Then Pasha sat back and thought for a moment. "I'll have some rice, if it pleases Your Majesty—some grains of rice."

"How many grains?"

"Well, give me two grains of rice for the first square on your chessboard, then four grains for the second square, sixteen for the third square, and so on up to the sixty-fourth square."

"A little rice doesn't seem much reward for the service you have given me."

"It will be quite enough for me," said Pasha.

A few days later, the king was called to the building where the grain was stored. This was a huge wooden structure, as big as a palace and filled to the rafters with rice. The harvest that year had been good. One of the king's advisers greeted him with a troubled look, saying, "Majesty, we do not have the rice to pay Pasha what you owe him."

"What? The place is bursting with rice."

"But see, I have done the calculations! After three squares of the chessboard, there are only sixteen grains of rice. After the fourth square, there are two hundred and fifty-six—still only a cupful. But just two squares later and the number is in the millions!" The poor man held out his arms most eloquently, as if to ask what he could do. "I'm sorry, Majesty, no one can deal with such numbers. After twenty squares, there are more grains than I can count. There is not enough rice in this kingdom or in the whole of the world to pay Pasha what you owe him."

Hmm, thought the king, who could almost hear Pasha saying, "Many littles make a lot." This was as neat a trick as could be. He sent for Pasha and rewarded him, not with rice, but with the position of first councillor. What better man to be in charge of the royal purse?

It can be a tricky thing, knowing
how far to trust people.

PEACE IS DECLARED

THERE WAS a fox long ago who loved hens—loved
to eat them, that is—and there was one hen he fancied
more than any other. She was large, red, fat, and—
sadly—awfully clever. The fox knew that he would
need a good plan to coax Red Hen away from the farmyard and into the woods, where she would be easy meat.

One day Red Hen was pecking away to her heart's
content when she saw the fox coming lickety-split. Up
she hopped onto the roof of a barn, where foxes fear to
tread.

"Come down!" cried the fox. "You'll never believe
what has happened. It's wonderful news."

"The news will sound just as good up here as down
there," replied Red Hen.

"But that's just it! The king has declared peace all over the kingdom. There is to be no more fighting. We must all be friends."

"Aaah," said Red Hen thoughtfully.

"Isn't it wonderful? Why don't you come down, and we can go for a walk in the woods together, just you and me!"

"Good news indeed," said Red Hen, craftily peering into the distance. "Here comes the farmer with his loaded gun. Why don't you tell him about . . ."

"About the peace?" she was going to say—but the fox was already over the hill and far away.

Your Collector of Stories suspects that we have all met the bully at the door or someone very like him. Some of us will have been the bully at the door.

THE BULLY AT THE DOOR

IN ONE small corner of the wide world, there was once a rich merchant who liked to buy unusual things. People came to him knowing that they would get a fair price for what they had to sell, and they brought all sorts of objects: many-knotted carpets, rare old books, nuggets of lapis lazuli, glazed pots, and even brightly colored birds in wicker baskets. Such a man was very useful to the townsfolk, especially when they needed cash in a hurry.

One day the merchant's bodyguard died after falling from his horse and had to be replaced by another man. This new bodyguard soon found a way of making himself rich. He stood outside the door and wouldn't let anyone in to see the merchant—not until they promised to give him half of whatever money they received.

"Some for you and some for me," he would say with a nasty grin. "Isn't that fair?"

All went well for the scoundrel until one day a peasant arrived with a beautiful fish to sell. It was a huge sturgeon, big enough for twenty people or more and certain to fetch a fine price.

"Half the money comes to me," the bodyguard said to the peasant, whose name was Otto. "Otherwise you can't go in."

"But it's my fish," said Otto.

"And my rules!" snarled the bodyguard. "If you know anybody else who'll pay you well for that fish, go and sell it to them."

There was no one else to buy the fish. Otto nodded, saying, "It's a deal, then. Half each."

"And keep this between you and me, or I'll finish you. And make sure I get what's coming to me."

"I'll do that," said Otto.

In he went. One look at the sturgeon was enough to make the merchant's mouth water, and he asked its price.

"Sir," said Otto, "the price of this fish is twenty blows upon my back with a good stout stick."

Somewhat puzzled, the merchant sat back to take a careful look at Otto through narrowed eyes. He suspected some trickery. "Why? Isn't it yours? Did you steal the fish?"

"No, sir, I caught it while bottom-fishing for eels."

"Then why are you asking me for a beating?"

"The fellow at the door says I am to give him half of what you are good enough to pay. I will gladly take ten strokes of the cane and leave the same to him."

Thus it came out that the bodyguard was crooked. The merchant, furious at the damage that such a man might do to his reputation, had the thief beaten and run out of town, while to Otto he gave a fair price for his fish.

Jesus was a teacher who spoke to his followers about right and wrong, and made them think.

THE GOOD SAMARITAN

ONE DAY a lawyer, hearing Jesus say that one must love and respect one's neighbor, asked the question, "Who, then, is my neighbor?"

So Jesus told the story of a man who was attacked by thieves as he went down from Jerusalem to Jericho. They stripped him, beat him, and made off with all that he had, leaving him half dead by the side of the road.

Soon afterward a priest came along the same road, but when he saw the victim lying there, he passed to the other side and made no effort to help. Then a Levite came to the place. He, too, looked at the wounded man and, like the priest, hurried away in case there was trouble.

It so happened that a Samaritan was making the journey to Jericho and took pity on the stranger. Kneeling by the roadside, he gave the man water, cleaned his wounds with oil and wine, and provided bandages for the worst of the cuts. Then he took the man to an inn so that he would be safe and warm in the night.

That wasn't all. In the morning, he gave two coins to the innkeeper, saying, "Take care of the stranger until he's well. If you spend more than I've given you, I'll repay you on my journey back."

At the end of the story, Jesus turned to the lawyer with a question of his own. "Which of those three do you think was a neighbor to the wounded stranger?"

"The one who took care of him."

Jesus nodded and said, "Go, then; be like the Samaritan, and do as he did."

THE MICE HOLD
A MEETING

THERE WAS a famous occasion when the Mice called a meeting to discuss what they should do about their common enemy, the Cat. Mice are mice, after all, and cats are cats. The problem was obvious.

All sorts of plans were put forward at this grand meeting, but the one that had most popular appeal was suggested by a young mouse.

"Our problem is," the Young Mouse said, "that we never know when the Cat is coming. It can sneak up on us because we don't know it's there. Why don't we put a bell around its neck? And then, when we hear the tinkling of the bell, we'll know that our enemy is near!"

Almost everyone decided that such a wonderful plan, such an obvious plan, should be agreed upon at

once. When the applause had died down, however, an old mouse rose to speak.

"I have just one question about this excellent idea." The Old Mouse paused and said, "Which one of us is going to put the bell around the neck of the cat?"

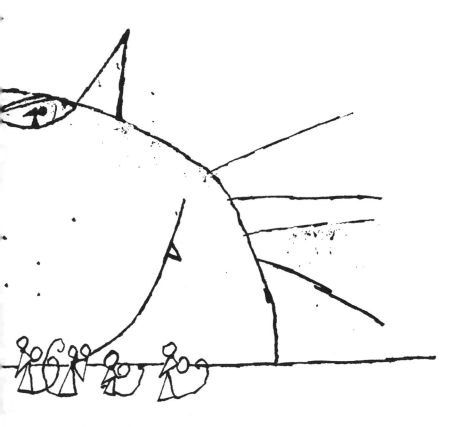

THE RAT CATCHER

OVER SEVEN HUNDRED years ago, according to the famous story, the town of Hamelin in northern Germany suffered a plague of rats. The creatures ran freely through the streets, in and out of the houses, eating all the food they could find by day and by night. The townsfolk set traps, put down poison, brought in cats and dogs, but it made no difference. There always seemed to be as many rats as before. Everyone had a horror story to tell about those vermin—some even said that babies were no longer safe in their cradles.

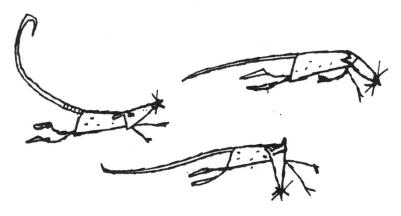

The mayor and his councillors had no idea what to do. They spent every council meeting talking about rats and wondering what to say to the people of Hamelin, who were angry and demanded action. They paid taxes, after all, and wanted something done. But what sort of action? The members of the council shook their worried heads and said, "What do we know about rats?"

Then one summer day, a stranger walked into Hamelin town and asked to speak to the mayor.

"If you pay me what I ask," he told the councillors, "I will get rid of your rats."

What an odd-looking fellow this was! Unusually tall and thin, he wore a long tunic made from colored squares of cloth, so that he resembled in some ways a harlequin. His eyes were blue and steady. He had long

fingers, which sometimes strayed to caress a musical pipe hanging from a cord around his neck.

"What is your price?" asked one of the councillors.

"A thousand guilders."

"We'll pay it," said the mayor, knowing he would have paid ten times that sum to be free of the scuttling hordes. "A thousand guilders to you when the job is done!"

Then the stranger stepped into the streets and started to play his pipe. What charm there was in that music no one has ever known, but from every street, from every private house and every public building in the town of Hamelin, the rats came rushing and tumbling

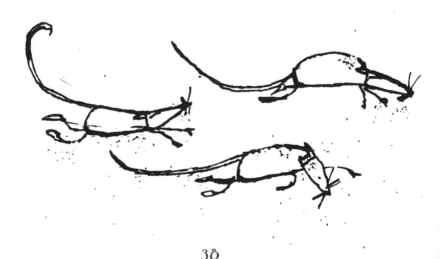

to follow the piper. Through the marketplace he led them, and beyond to where the river Weser flowed near the edge of town. The rats plunged into the Weser and drowned. As far as anyone could tell, not one of the beasts survived.

A little later, while the steeple bells were still ringing in celebration, the piper came to ask for his money. This time the councillors were not so inclined to take him seriously. Did he really expect to be given such a sum for an hour's work? Hadn't the river actually done the job by drowning the

rats? And besides, could anyone really be sure that every single rat was dead?

"Come, my friend," said the mayor, "forget the thousand guilders. Take fifty!"

"We agreed a price," replied the piper.

But they wouldn't pay. The fellow was no more than a wandering minstrel, a gypsy type who would take their hard-earned money and spend it somewhere far away from here. Besides, the rats were dead. The job was done, could not be undone.

"You will pay me," said the piper as he left. "You may keep your precious gold—but I will be paid."

Before long, the music of the pipe was heard again in Hamelin. This time, out of the houses, rushing and tumbling to follow the piper, came the children of the town. Whatever charm was in the music made them dance and sing—but the people seeing them go by found that the opposite was true for themselves: they could only watch as if time itself had slowed. The children skipped and laughed their way through the marketplace and beyond—toward the river Weser.

At the last moment, the piper turned away from the river toward the Koppelberg Hill. It seemed that now and at last he must stop—and the little ones, too—for the Koppelberg rose steep and sheer to a great height. But as the piper approached, lo and behold the very mountainside split open, and through the chasm stepped the piper and all the children of Hamelin.

I say "all," but there was one boy who, being lame, could not keep up with the others. For some moments, he had a glimpse of what he described as a wondrous land; then the hole in the mountainside closed before he could go through, and there was only solid rock before his eyes. He was obliged to turn back, the only one to come home.

The mayor sent out messages to all points of the compass: "A fortune to you, Piper, if only you come back and bring the children with you!" Sadly for the people of Hamelin, the stranger made no reply, and they never saw their children again.

NOT SPEAKING

WHAT A RIDICULOUS thing it is to be "not speaking," yet it happens to us all. It happened to a man and wife who lived in a Hungarian forest about two hundred years ago. During an argument, the front door of their cottage blew open in a gale, and neither of them would agree to shut it. (Most arguments are like that—extremely silly.) They decided that the first one to speak would have to shut the door. A sort of "trial of wills," you see.

Well, some time went by. Neither of them spoke, so the door stayed open. It was springtime in the natural world, but they couldn't see the beauty of the young buds and the flowers and the infinite shades of green—there was a battle to be won!

Neither of them shut the door, so one night a horde of mice came in and ate their way through some sacks of flour. Those mice left by the same open door they came in by, feeling well satisfied—the luckiest mice in the country.

Did he speak or she speak? Did one say, "The mice have eaten our flour"? Did either give in and shut the door?

No.

On the following afternoon, a lone wolf came slinking by, attracted by the open door. With no bother at all, he made off with all the fish drying in the smoke from the kitchen fire.

Did he speak or she speak? Did one say, "All our smoked fish have gone"? Did either give in and close the door? Not one bit.

Then from the depths of the forest on a moonlit night came a great brown bear, stooping to enter by the unshut door. She thrashed about, looking for all the newly baked bread and dried fruit she could find. Standing fully eight feet tall, she pulled a plank here and knocked a beam there, until at last . . . well, the walls fell down, the roof fell in, and there was no cottage left—not even an open door.

The husband and wife sat up in their bed, thankful to have escaped injury, and they gazed in amazement at the stars. Who first spoke to whom we do not know, but let us hope that each was thinking, *It would have been better if I had said something. I should have shut the door.*

**You can go from rags to riches in this life,
and you can go from riches to rags.**

THINGS COULD
BE WORSE

ONCE THERE WAS a very rich man who lived according to his wealth. In other words, he had the best of everything. His house was a mansion set in five hundred acres of farmland. His wife and children ate the finest foods and wore the latest clothes. When the family went up to town, they traveled in a coach painted blue and green and pulled by white horses, and ordinary folk would pause to watch the gentry go by.

One day, trying to become even richer, the rich man risked his money on an important business deal that went wrong. He lost his fine mansion, his farm, his easy life. Now he was forced to become a shopkeeper and live in a modest house at the edge of town. In time he became used to his situation, for he still had three acres of land and the family had more than enough to eat, but he couldn't help thinking back to those prosperous years when he lived in the lap of luxury.

Some years went by, and once more there came a stroke of bad luck. His shop burned down, and up in smoke went almost everything that he owned. He sold his acres of land, bought a horse and a wagon, and became a common carter. People hired him to carry things from here to there in his wagon. Now he no longer thought back to the days when he lived in a mansion. "How well I used to live when I was a shopkeeper!" he cried. "I had my profits and my little bit of land. Now see what I am reduced to—an ordinary carter!"

His new life was not so bad, though. One of his children left home—one less mouth to feed—and his wife took in washing to make a few extra pennies. Then misfortune struck again. The horse broke a leg in a pothole and had to be put down. Realizing that he could never afford to buy another horse, the carter decided that there was only one thing to be done: become a porter. In other words, carry things himself. And now, in weather good and bad, he was to be seen about the town, doubled up beneath a heavy load, and all for the price of a loaf.

One wet afternoon, as he carried a gentleman's suitcase across the street, the gentleman recognized him, for he had known the porter long ago.

"Is it you, my friend? But what happened to you? Where's your mansion, your money, your five hundred acres? When I knew you, you had a painted coach and horses—now you're carrying luggage across the street!"

"Say no more about mansions and money," said the porter. "I've long forgotten those. What I remember are the wonderful days when I had a horse—and was a carter."

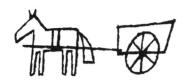

You will sometimes hear people say,
"Flattery will get you nowhere."
Well, sometimes they are right.

FINE WORDS

IN A TIME before this, there was a great city within a circle of walls. The governor of this city was a wealthy prince who was in his palace one day when a knock happened at the door.

It was the knock of a wandering poet. He asked for permission to say some verses in praise of the prince. The chancellor waved him away with the words, "Can't you see we're busy?" But the prince laid down his pen.

"No, no, we're only signing some papers. Come in, Master Poet; let us hear what you want to say."

Thus encouraged, the poet began to recite a sonnet that contained some wonderful phrases. The prince was said to be beyond compare—he had the power of the bear, the will of the lion, the leopard's speed, and the far-seeing eye of the hawk.

"Great stuff," cried the prince. "Obviously a reward is called for. What do these fine words cost nowadays, my friend?"

The chancellor scowled, for he did not believe in wasting money on poets, while the poet himself gave an eloquent shrug of his shoulders as if to leave the problem to the prince.

"One hundred dinars!" said the prince, naming a goodly sum.

"O Your most noble Majesty!" cried the poet, launching himself into another sonnet. In this one, the beauty of the prince was said to be beyond compare— he was as fair as the sunset, as beguiling as the moon, as welcome as summer rain, and as fresh as the fern in spring. And when he had finished, the prince cried, "Wonderful! Let him have five hundred dinars!"

The poor chancellor winced with pain, for five hundred dinars could buy a Thoroughbred stallion or a vineyard. The poet—unable to believe his luck— immediately embarked on yet another sonnet, this time in praise of the prince's power.

"One thousand dinars!" cried the prince.

At this point, the chancellor took the poet by the elbow and steered him to the door, saying, "Wait out there for your money." Then he returned to speak his mind to the prince. "Sire, forgive my boldness, but at this rate of pay for poets, you're going to make us poor. One dinar would have done that wordsmith, and you have given him a thousand!"

"Really?"

"I heard you, my lord. The fellow was in ecstasy every time you mentioned money. It was like poetry to his ears."

"Calm yourself, Chancellor. I'll give to him what he gave to me—fine words."

The chancellor wiped his troubled brow. "I don't quite follow you."

"Am I not supposed to be as brave as a lion and as fair as a sunset? Such wonderful nonsense! Well, fine words deserve fine words. I hope mine made our poet as happy as his made me!"

"Then . . . I needn't pay him with dinars?"

"Of course not! Did he mean a word of what he said? No. And neither do I. He gave me the empty words of a poet; I give him the empty promise of a prince."

You will sometimes hear people say,
"Flattery will get you nowhere."
Well, sometimes they are wrong.

KING OF THE AIR

A KEEN-EYED FOX spotted a crow up a tree with a tasty piece of cheese in his beak. The fox, quickly thinking up a trick to get the cheese for herself, stood under the tree and said, "Aha! This must be that good-looking crow that everyone is talking about. At last I've seen him for myself."

The crow hardly bothered to look down at first, for he was a proud young fellow and it was his nature to be scornful.

"What a noble creature he is, to be sure," the fox went on. "Those feathers are the smoothest I have ever seen. And the head—well, the head is perfect."

The crow hopped along the branch, the better to be seen. It was pleasing to hear so many nice things said about oneself, even if they came from a creature who couldn't fly. He gave a quick flick of his tail feathers to show them off; and all the while the cheese remained firmly in his beak.

"Best of all are the eyes, I think," the fox said. "They have the dark shine of precious stones. The only thing I cannot praise is his voice, which I have not heard. If that crow sings as sweetly as he looks, then he is chief among birds and King of the Air."

The crow, bewitched by these remarks and wanting to believe them, opened his beak to show off his singing voice. He gave a loud caw, down fell the cheese, and the fox said, "You do indeed have a voice, dear Crow, but you are sadly lacking in brains."

BIG SQUEEZER AND LITTLE TOUGH GUYS

JIMBA LINN and his friends were children who lived near the Magic River.

Everyone who lived near the Magic River knew Big Squeezer well. Big Squeezer was a long, slow, fat snake who swallowed her meals whole and then hung down from the trees in loops.

Snakes are rarely popular, of course. Some of them, like the yellow river serpent, are quick and deadly. But Big Squeezer never did any harm to people, so the children were allowed to reply if she spoke to them.

One day in the swamplands, she spoke to Jimba Linn and his friends. "I would like to be yellow all over instead of green and black," she said. "Go to the village and bring some paint. But remember, it must be yellow."

Jimba Linn and his friends did as they were told, for after all it was just as much fun to make Big Squeezer yellow as to capture frogs and toads. They returned with some bright paint made from yellow clay.

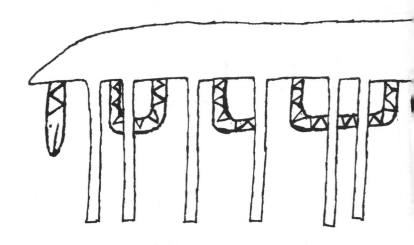

"Why do you want to be yellow?" Jimba Linn asked while he painted.

"Because I am long and slow and fat, and I have no prestige. I want to be feared like the yellow river serpent. I want to be a great and significant snake."

Soon the job was done, and Big Squeezer was well pleased with the change in her appearance. However, when she hung down from the trees in yellow loops, people made fun of her. Some called her "Big Yellow" and smiled among themselves as they did so. Others asked her to give them a talk on the importance of being yellow. No one was afraid of her.

Only Jimba Linn saw how this teasing disappointed the long, slow, fat snake. "I know how you feel, Big

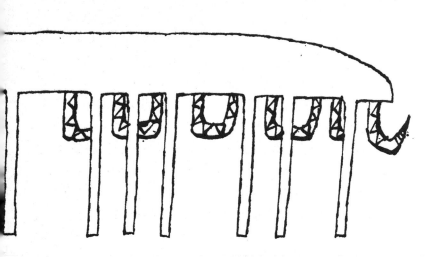

Squeezer," he said, "but you mustn't worry about it. You have given them a reason to smile, and people always have a soft spot for those who make them smile."

Those words were no comfort to Big Squeezer, who saw that being a great and significant snake wasn't only a matter of being the right color—there were also certain things you must do. So she crept up on a carpenter while he was making a door frame and squeezed him to death.

The effects of this action were seen at once. Mothers rushed out and plucked dusty children from their games. Frightened people muttered in doorways and there was no more cheerful talk about the importance of being yellow. Everyone avoided Big Squeezer, who hung down from the trees in loops feeling powerful, and significant, and splendidly alone.

By nightfall, though, the hunters had gathered in groups. And when they came after Big Squeezer with nets and knives and cries of hate, she was fortunate to reach the swamplands in one piece.

Now she saw what a mistake she had made. A terrible danger hung over her. At sunrise her spirits lifted when she saw that the yellow paint had come off in the water, and she said to herself, *I will show them that I am the same as I used to be.*

But they were waiting for her in the morning light, and even though she was no longer yellow, they still saw her as a great and significant snake. Within minutes, Big Squeezer was dead and skinned.

Sometimes, when children pretend to be little tough guys, their parents say to them, "You'd better be happy with the way you are, or you'll end up like Big Squeezer."

THE GOLDEN TOUCH

ONCE THERE WAS a king on this earth who did a good turn for one of the gods. The name of the king was Midas, and the name of the god was Bacchus. In return for the favor, Bacchus said that Midas could have a wish come true—whatever wish he wanted.

Now, Midas was a man of great riches and wealth, the sort of man who collected precious stones, jewels, and gold. He liked gold so much that he would spend hours polishing his coins with a soft cloth to make them shine.

"I would like whatever I touch to turn into gold," he said.

"Are you sure that's what you want?" asked Bacchus.

"Certain! How could there be such a thing as too much gold?"

"Then I grant what you ask," smiled Bacchus. "You have the golden touch."

At first Midas was doubtful; but he touched a twig on a nearby tree, and it turned to gold. Then a laurel leaf, a blade of grass, stone . . . all still in the very shape they used to be, but gold.

Midas looked to the heavens in wonder, unable to believe he had the most powerful gift on earth. Running to a beach nearby, the king scooped up a handful of sand and let it trickle through his fingers. Every grain of sand now glittered, and every grain was gold.

Truly, he had the golden touch.

To celebrate his newfound power, the king ordered his cooks to prepare a banquet. His family and friends came to the table, where presently Midas hoped to show off his gift, but his gift soon showed itself. He plucked a grape from a bunch; it turned to gold. The cup he reached for did the same, and that knife, that plate, that napkin—all gold!

All at once, Midas saw that he had no choice in the matter, for whatever he touched was bound to change whether he willed it or not. Was this what he wanted— for the world he lived in to turn to metal? One of his children came toward him, laughing, and Midas saw with his mind's eye what might happen if he were to cuddle the child in his usual way. Up he rose from the table, horrified   and ran.

He ran to the place where Bacchus had granted his deadly wish and explained what had happened to him. "I can't enjoy the things that are natural," he cried out to Bacchus, "not even a drink of water or the embrace of my children. These things are priceless; they cannot be bought. If you pity me, take back your gift and let me be the way I was."

Sometimes the gods of ancient times were merciful; sometimes they couldn't give tuppence for what happened to mortals like you and me. Midas was lucky. Bacchus sent him to bathe in a river of freshwater, after which he lost not only the golden touch, but also any fondness he ever had for that yellow metal.

THE STICK OF TRUTH

IN THE CENTRAL square of a great city, there stood the statue of a famous general. This bronze soldier was mounted on a horse with two silver stirrups. Early one morning, a boy climbed up and stole the left stirrup, an act that offended and enraged the public. However, the crime was seen by a street cleaner and some others, and before long four boys had been brought before the governor.

Now, the governor had no idea which boy was the guilty one, for the thief didn't own up. So he sent for a well-known judge, admitting that he was not sure what to do. "I cannot let them go, for one is the thief. Yet I am unwilling to punish them all, for three of them are innocent. What would you advise in this situation?"

It was a dilemma the judge understood well: should one punish them all, including the innocent? Or free them all, including the guilty? Experience had taught him a way to proceed. It sometimes worked. He turned to his assistant and said, "Bring me my red bag, the one with the stick of truth in it. I don't think we have a great problem here."

When the bag arrived, the judge drew out four sticks, all sharpened at one end, and each exactly the same length as the others. The judge gave one stick to each boy, telling him to bring it back the following morning. "One of you is the thief who stole the stirrup," he said, "and the thief has the stick of truth. It will show him up."

The governor was puzzled. "But how does this work?" he asked.

The judge addressed the boys in front of him. "One of you four has the stick of truth. When you bring back the sticks in the morning, the stick of truth will be just a little longer than the others—about a thumbnail longer. That's how we'll know the thief." The judge waved a hand at the boys. "So off you go until the morning."

When the morning came, they assembled once more, and in the midst of a great silence, the boys presented their sticks to the judge. Holding up the sticks, he measured them against one another and found that one was shorter than its fellows by about a thumbnail.

"This boy here, who presented the shorter stick, is the guilty one," said the judge.

"But you said it would be longer," the governor pointed out.

"So I did. And our thief decided to whittle away a bit of his stick, just in case. Now that his own conscience has betrayed him, I trust he will lead us to the missing stirrup."

Then the boy confessed, fetched the stirrup from its hiding place down a drain, and agreed on his punishment: that he should keep the statue of the general clean of dust and pigeon droppings for the rest of that year.

THE MONEY HAT

THERE WAS a man in Ireland who went to the Lammas Fair one time, where he made some money buying and selling horses. Now, he didn't want to walk around all day with the money in his pocket, so this is what he did. He went into a tavern and said, "Landlord, would you keep fifty pounds for me?"

The landlord said that he would.

"And, landlord," said the man, "when I come back, I'll raise my hat and say to you, 'Do you remember the man in the hat with the peacock's feather?' Then you'll know to give me back my money. There'll be a shilling or two for your good self, of course."

"All right," said the landlord.

He did the same thing at two more taverns—so now there were three landlords each holding fifty pounds for our man in the hat.

Soon he fell in with a carpenter, and they went for a sip of stout together. Our man said to the landlord, "Do you remember the man in the hat with the peacock's feather?"

"I do certainly," said the landlord. "I've got fifty pounds for the man in that hat."

The carpenter was very impressed when he saw the fifty pounds handed over. Then they went to another tavern, and our man said to the landlord, "Do you remember the man in the hat with the peacock's feather?"

"I do," said the landlord, "and there's fifty pounds for him."

When this happened at yet another tavern, the carpenter took our man to one side and asked him in a serious way, "How exactly does that hat work?"

"It's a money hat," our man explained. "There aren't many about, I can tell you."

"Do you think it would work for anybody?"

"I'd say it might."

"Do you think it might work for me?"

"I'd say it would. Money hats aren't fussy. But I couldn't agree to part with it for less than one hundred pounds."

"I'll buy it," said the carpenter.

Our man hurried off with the hundred pounds. The carpenter put on his newly purchased hat, went into a tavern, and smiled at the landlord, saying, "Do you remember the man in the hat with the peacock's feather?"

"Can't say I do," replied the landlord, looking at him strangely. "What about him?"

"I thought you might have something for him."

"Something like what?"

"Fifty pounds," said the carpenter with a wink, "for the man in the hat."

"Fifty pounds, is it!" declared the landlord. "I've got the toe of my boot for him if he's not through that door in ten seconds flat!"

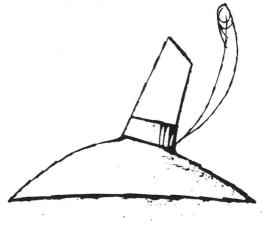

MAKING THE JOURNEY

IN DAYS GONE BY, when many things were different but human nature was the same, there was a king who had four advisers. Now the king listened to the opinions of all his advisers, but as time went by he came to rely more and more on the opinion of one of them, so that the other three grew jealous. "If this goes on," they whispered to one another, "the king will feel that he doesn't need us at all. We might as well go and live with the common people and become butchers and bakers!" This thought—that they might lose their power and privileges—helped them to make up their minds: their colleague, Kapsan, must die.

They were clever men, and the plan they devised to get rid of Kapsan was a good one. This is what happened. The first one went to the king, saying, "Your Highness, I had a dream last night in which your father spoke to me."

"But my father is dead," said the king.

"I know that, Your Majesty. But in this dream your father told me to tell you that he has a problem in his next life. You are to send him your most trusted adviser to help him with his affairs."

Of this strange dream the king took little notice—until later in the day another adviser came to him, saying, "I saw your father in a dream, Your Majesty. He was in a beautiful place on the other side. Only . . . he asks you to send him your chief adviser, for he is having some difficulties."

When the third of the conspirators came to the king saying much the same thing, he actually mentioned Kapsan by name and said that he was wanted for a short while in the world beyond the grave.

Nothing so strange had ever happened to the king before, and yet he suspected neither treachery nor lies. *If three people have the same dream,* he said to himself, *it must be true.* Kapsan must die; how else could he make the journey to the other side and help his dead father? With a heavy heart, he went to break this news to his most trusted adviser.

Kapsan listened to what the king related to him and grew most thoughtful. Then he said, "If my former master wishes to see me, then of course I must go.

However, may I ask for this favor—give me seven days to settle my earthly affairs, and then if it pleases Your Majesty, allow me to be buried alive in the tomb of my ancestors."

These terms were granted. After seven days Kapsan was enclosed within the family tomb, which was then sealed; in order to leave nothing to chance, his three former colleagues put guards around it night and day. Their clever plan, it seemed, had met with the success it deserved.

But they hadn't been quite clever enough. During the seven days, the most trusted of Kapsan's servants had been tunneling under the ground, making an escape route from the sealed tomb to a piece of unused land close by. Within an hour of his interment, Kapsan was back in his own house, where he remained for one week behind shuttered windows.

Then he dressed himself in clean white linen, put on his badges of office, and went to see his master, the king. The time was well chosen, for at the end of a good meal the king had surrounded himself with his family, their guests, and, of course, his three advisers. A great shout went up as Kapsan entered the banquet hall—a chorus of acclamation and wonder. Where had he been, what had he seen, how did he make the awesome journey home, and what words could he say of Paradise?

"My father!" cried the king. "What news do you have of him?"

Kapsan possessed the gifts of an orator and the vision of a poet, and he skillfully produced answers to all their questions.

"Your father is well, my lord King," he said. "I was able to help him, but not as much as I had hoped. He now feels that three heads are sure to be better than one and asks that you send to him my three colleagues over there. He would like to see them now—today—for the matter has become quite urgent."

In this way, the three advisers were sent to make the journey they had planned for Kapsan; and they did not return.

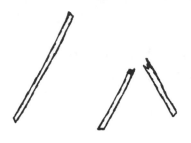

DIVIDED WE FALL

THE YOUNG MEN of a certain tribe could not live peacefully with one another. They called each other names, quarreled over work, and fought at the dinner table like sparrows squabbling for crumbs. Their chieftain dreaded to think what might happen after his death, when there would be no one to keep them under control.

One day the chieftain asked each of the young men to bring along a stick to dinner. He collected up the sticks, lashed them together with twine, and invited each youth to break the bundle across his knee. They tried and failed.

Then the chieftain untied the bundle, handed each youth a single stick, and asked him to break it in two. None had any difficulty in doing so.

"As with sticks, so with people," the chieftain warned. "Those who quarrel and stand alone are easily broken, like single sticks. But those who stand together will be a match for their enemies."

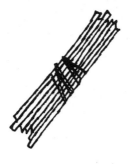

The decisions you make now will have consequences later in life — as the king of the jungle found out in a famous story.

THE LION AND THE MOUSE

A SLEEPY LION, while resting one day in the shade, was wakened by a mouse running over his face. Trapping the mouse under his paw, the lion was about to crush the little creature, when it began to beg for its life.

"Please let me go," said the squeaky voice. "What can it matter to a great one like you whether I live or die? And if you spare my life, I will repay you one day for your kindness."

On hearing this, the lion burst out laughing, for he could not imagine what a mouse could do for a lion. But the little fellow had amused him, and, besides, it was far too small to eat, so he let the mouse go.

There came a day when the lion found himself trapped in a net left by some hunters. The more he struggled, the more the net gathered him in, and for all his great strength, the lion could only lie there helplessly and roar. Among those who heard the roars of the lion was the little mouse whose life he had spared. It ran to the scene, gnawed through the net with its teeth, and managed to set the lion free.

"There!" said the little one. "You laughed at me once, but the mouse has done for the lion what the lion did for the mouse."

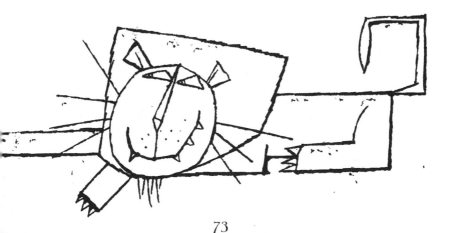

73

My father used to say to me,
"Will you use your common sense!"
Perhaps he knew about the frog called:

ONE~TIME WISE

A SOCIETY of friends met from time to time in an old hay barn. They were an owl, a fox, a farmyard cat, and a frog. Although they were friends, this was not a society of equals, for the owl regarded herself as intellectually superior to the other three. Owl had flown across the sea, had visited far countries, and could tell many a tale about what happened there. She was therefore known as A Thousand Times Wise.

The fox, famous for his quiet cunning, had been to the nearest big town several times and often spoke about its bright lights and noisy streets. He was known as A Hundred Times Wise.

Then there was Cat, or Ten Times Wise. He could tell a thing or two about life in the local village and knew all the latest gossip.

Finally came Frog. She was thought to have a less-than-average sort of brain and was therefore known as One-Time Wise.

As the friends were having some conversation late one summer afternoon, a smoky haze began to fill the air. With a crackle and a roar, a blazing fire broke out among the hay bales and spread through the barn with terrifying speed. What was to be done?

"We will be all right!" said A Thousand Times Wise, flapping up and down on the spot. "I can think of a thousand ways to deal with this crisis."

"Oh, I'm used to this," declared A Hundred Times Wise. "I know of a hundred things to do when there's a fire."

"Me, too," cried Ten Times Wise, almost choking in the heat. "I can easily think up ten good answers to our present problem."

They may have been expecting some sort of comment from their other friend, but she wasn't there. One-Time Wise could think of only one thing to do: she bolted for the nearest door at the first whiff of smoke.

Frog sat outside, blinking at the flames, watching the barn burn down and wondering whether the society of friends would ever meet again.

Greedy people who think they can smell money
are easily led by the nose.

THE SECOND BAG
OF GOLD

IN DAYS GONE BY, there was a man who collected
taxes for the government. Now it happened that this
tax collector had to spend the night in a strange town,
which worried him, for he had a bag of one hundred
gold pieces hidden away in the deepest pocket of his
cloak.

I can't trust anyone in this place, he thought. *I'll hide
the money rather than keep it on me, just in case.*

Choosing a quiet spot near the wall of the old town,
he scooped out a hole in soft ground and tucked the
money away. He had no idea that a stonemason's wife
had seen him through a tiny window in her gable wall.
She and her husband dug up the money as soon as the
tax collector had gone.

The sight of that empty hole in the morning
shocked the tax collector to the heels of his boots. Those

hundred pieces were the government's gold, and he would have to answer for them. This meant prison for sure—or maybe worse. Many a false servant of the government had ended up dangling from a rope. "But no one saw me bury the money!" he cried out loud.

That was when he noticed the tiny window in the gable wall, a window he had not seen in yesterday's hurry. So it was possible, then, that he had been watched. . . . And if so, someone in that house was the likely thief. As he went around to the front of the house, a plan was forming in his mind. He rapped on the door.

The stonemason opened it.

"I'm a stranger in this town, my friend," said the tax collector, "and I have a problem."

"What's that to do with me?" replied the stone-mason.

"Well, you were recommended to me as a wise man who gives good advice. I came to this town with two bags of gold. Yesterday I safely buried the first bag, to halve the chances of my being robbed—one must be careful, after all. But the second bag is becoming a nuisance. What shall I do with it? Must I keep it with me? Do you think I should bury it in the same hole as the other gold or find a new hiding place? Maybe you know an honest man who would look after it for me?"

The door of the house opened wider as the stone-mason's wife appeared. With a smile, she invited the tax collector to step into the shade of the hall, adding, "I couldn't help overhearing what you were saying to my husband. We wouldn't advise you to trust anyone with your money—would we, dear?"

"No," grunted her husband.

"And why bother with a new hiding place?" the wife went on. "If it's good enough for one bag of gold, why not two? Much more convenient! Put it with the other one."

"I'm sure you're right," said the tax collector. "Thank you for your advice; I shall bury the other bag tonight."

As soon as the man had gone, the wife turned to her husband. "We must put back his bag of gold before he finds that it's missing."

"Why?"

"Because, if he finds that his first bag has gone, he won't put the second bag there. Don't you see? We're going to get both bags. Just think—two hundred gold pieces!"

So they replaced the gold, unaware that this time someone was watching them. It was a relieved tax collector who came to dig up his money a little while later. Then he left that town, vowing never to set foot in the place again.

A FINE BALANCE

A MOTHER LOUSE and her family of young lice lived in the bed of a noble lady. They drank the blood of the lady every night as she lay peacefully asleep. They were a happy bunch of parasites who knew how to avoid trouble. They never drank too much blood, and they never bit the noble lady at an inappropriate time or in an inappropriate place. She had no idea that she was breakfast, lunch, and dinner to her undemanding, unambitious, microscopic guests.

One night a young flea arrived in the bed—a most unwelcome visitor. The mother louse told him to go away at once, for she knew that he was dangerous. "This is our place," she said. "You have no business coming here to make life difficult for us."

The flea was on his best behavior and spoke softly. "You'll find that I'm no bother at all. Please let me stay and feed from time to time. There is enough blood for all of us, and more."

"No, you'll bite at the wrong moment, or too deeply, or in the wrong place! You are sure to upset the fine balance that we lice understand so well. You must go."

"Where to?" said the flea. "The wind blew me here; there's nowhere else I can go. Please—teach me what to do and I will not let you down."

At last the mother louse relented and agreed to let the flea remain in the noble lady's bed. "Do only what I tell you," she warned. "To begin with, you may bite her on the toes, but only when she is deep asleep or drowsy with wine. Above all, obey the golden rule: Never draw attention to yourself."

The flea, however, being young and impatient, soon tired of toes. One evening he bit the noble lady on the neck before she had even fallen asleep. Up she rose, calling for her maidservants, who searched the bed most thoroughly and soon disposed of the brash young flea and the undemanding, unambitious, microscopic lice.

FAIR WARNING

THERE GOES a story that a man helped a stranger one dark night.

The man who did the favor was a young man. The stranger looked at him and said, "I must thank you for your help. Men and women know me as . . . Death. I take people on the journey from this life to whatever lies beyond."

"If you are Death, you are to be feared," replied the young man.

"Feared by some, welcomed by others. In my own right, I am neither good nor bad. You have helped me tonight, and so I grant you fair warning. Death shall not call on you unannounced; there will be no sudden surprise. I will send you my Messengers. Until we meet again . . . farewell."

The young man went on his way. As the years passed by like so many candles on a cake, he was a well man. Of course, there were occasions when a fever came, and he tossed and turned through restless nights;

or a toothache threatened him with poison; or he had an accident that required the setting of a bone. But he had no great worry about such things, for he reasoned that Death had promised him fair warning.

He became a painter of considerable reputation and wealth. Now that his best years were behind him, he saw wrinkles in the mirror, wore glasses to read, and used a walking stick to get to the top of the house where the light was good. Yet always he remembered the Messengers: he would know.

There came an evening when the man felt something at his shoulder: a kind of presence that could not be shrugged away. When he looked, it was as if the clock had been turned back to a moment long ago, for there in front of him—quite unchanged—stood the stranger called Death.

"You must follow me. It's time to make the journey now."

"Now? But my family and my friends! I must have the chance to say good-bye."

"No."

"What about my work? I'm an artist. You must understand that my best work may be yet to come. I can't just stop."

"What's done is done," was the reply.

"But your promise, your fair warning, your Messengers!"

Then Death turned to him calmly and said, "There have been many messengers. Each new wrinkle in the skin, for example. Each night's sleep, like a little death. Every fever. Every lost tooth. Forgetfulness. The gray in your beard. The glasses that you wear for reading. Even this." Saying which, Death held high the walking stick with the ivory handle. "Could you not see that this was a sign from me to you?"

Then Death paused and gave a final nod. "The place is here and the time is now."

APPOINTMENT IN SAMARKAND

ONE MORNING, a nobleman burst into the court of a wise and elderly king, saying, "Pity me, great lord, I have just seen Azrael in the courtyard below. He stared at me with a long, strange look, an angry look, and I am afraid."

Now Azrael was the angel of death, a collector of souls. He brought people from this world into the next. The nobleman feared that Azrael had come for him.

"What do you want me to do?" asked the king. In his view, what must be, must be.

"Lend me two horses, Majesty. If I leave now and make good speed, I could get far away from here—perhaps even to the city of Samarkand."

The horses were given, for the king saw that nothing could prevent the man from trying to prolong his life. He felt obliged to flee. And besides, the king believed that kindness was an end in itself.

Later that day, the king himself spoke to Azrael, the angel of death, with whom he sometimes discussed matters of the mind.

"Why did you look so long and hard at my noble friend this morning?" asked the king. "He claims you gave him an angry look."

"I am never angry," said Azrael. "I was only amazed to see him here, for I have an appointment with him tomorrow—in Samarkand."

TRUST

A FATHER TORTOISE, a mother tortoise, and a baby tortoise decided to go on a picnic. They collected all the usual things, such as bananas and tomatoes and cucumber sandwiches, and also cans of apricots and baked beans. They were especially careful to remember the baked beans, for that was their favorite food. After a month or so, they were ready, and they set off for the beach. Baby Tortoise took his bathing suit in case the sun came out and he got the chance to swim.

So they walked and walked, and they walked some more, until a year went by and they sat down for a rest. Then off they started again until two years went by, and they reached the beach where they planned to have the picnic. In no time at all, Mother Tortoise had the stuff out of the baskets and spread out on a rug. Very nice it looked, too. Father Tortoise wondered whether he should start with canned apricots or baked beans. Then . . .

"Oh no!" cried Father Tortoise. "How could we be so stupid? We've forgotten the can opener!"

Such misery. They looked everywhere, but it was true. No can opener. Mother Tortoise and Father Tortoise looked at Baby Tortoise and said, "You could run back for it, little one."

"Me?"

"Nothing else to do," said Father Tortoise. "We can't have a proper picnic without that can opener."

"All right, then, I'll go," said Baby. "But you have to promise me something. Promise you won't touch a thing until I come back."

"Do you think we would start without you?" said Mother Tortoise. "We'd never be so mean; of course we promise."

So Baby started on the journey back. A year went by, and Mother and Father began to feel a bit hungry; but they had promised not to start eating, so they didn't. A second year went by, and then a third.

"Maybe we could have a sandwich each," said Mother Tortoise. "He'd never know."

"We should wait until he comes back," said Father Tortoise.

Another year went by. "That's four years," said Father Tortoise, who was definitely feeling hungry by now. "Do you think he would mind if we had a bit of banana each?"

"We'd better have something while we're waiting, or I'm going to faint," said Mother Tortoise.

So they opened a banana. They were just about to bite into the sweet lovely softness when a little voice said, "Aha, I knew you'd cheat!" Baby Tortoise popped out from the rock where he'd been hiding. "It's a good thing I didn't go back for that can opener," he said.

Your Collector of Stories is fond of a tale about the
Buddha, who was known as Siddhartha as a boy.
How refreshing to read about someone who
refuses to be violent.

SAVING A SWAN

YOUNG SIDDHARTHA was an active child, strong
and fit, with an intelligent mind and a lively imagina-
tion. He had a fine understanding of the needs of people
and animals. He was popular, too, although for some
reason one of his cousins disliked him intensely. The
cousin's name was Deva. Siddhartha had no idea why
Deva disliked him so much, and it is quite possible that
Deva didn't know either.

Early one morning, Deva shot a beautiful swan out
of the air with an arrow. The stricken bird fell to the
ground near Siddhartha, who ran to it, pulled out the
arrow, and tried to comfort it as best he could.

Then Deva arrived. "What do you think you're
doing with my swan? I shot it!"

"I know you did," said Siddhartha, "and I'm trying to save it. If the swan dies, it belongs to you, since you wanted to kill it. But if it lives, it's mine."

Neither boy would give in to the other, so their argument had to be taken to a court of law. In the meantime, Siddhartha kept the bird with him and gave it the best of care. By the time the judges decided in his favor, the swan had made a complete recovery, and Siddhartha set it free.

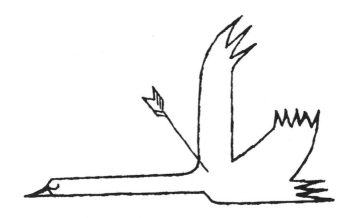

LANGUAGE AND THE PURSUIT OF TRUTH

A TEACHER and her students were interrupted by an important visitor—a man of politics—who looked at the blackboard where the teacher had been writing.

"But surely that word is not correct," cried the visitor. "Let me spell it for you."

Whereupon he rubbed out the word "quandary" and replaced it with "quandry."

The teacher smiled and accepted the correction with every show of grace. When the visitor had left, the students asked their teacher why she had accepted the correction, for they knew that "quandary" was the proper spelling. Surely she should have objected?

"Why?" the teacher replied mildly.

"Should we not insist upon truth in language?" someone observed.

After a pause, the teacher said, "Our visitor thought that he was helping me, and the wish to help is something to value in itself. Besides, this was a social occasion, requiring a light touch. I grant you, the pursuit of truth is sometimes so important that it overrides politeness and almost everything else; but whether our visitor can spell 'quandary' is neither here nor there."

A secret is a powerful thing, as two
young rascals discovered to their cost.

THE POWER OF
SECRETS

THEY LIVED in a small town in the mountains. One
was the son of the mayor, and the other was the schoolmaster's son. Now, the mayor wanted his son to learn
the arts of government and become a politician, while
the schoolmaster wanted his son to study his books and
become a lawyer. The boys themselves had no idea
what they wanted to become, nor did they care. They
had no interest in politics or law—they loved hawks,
horses, and hunting. They spent their days chasing
things. If they discovered a creature in the woods with
wings to fly or legs to run, they killed it if they could.
Then they came home and ate as if food was a new
thing they had discovered that morning.

Oh, the mothers scolded and the fathers shouted,
but the sons showed no sign of becoming sensible
young men. At last the mayor and the schoolmaster

decided that the boys must be separated, for they were a bad influence on each other.

The boys just laughed.

"You expect me to hunt alone?" said one.

"Everyone needs a friend to rely on," said the other.

They paid no attention to their parents and carried on as usual.

So the mayor and the schoolmaster let it be known that they would give a reward to anyone who could break up the friendship between the boys. Several people tried to win the reward but failed. Their methods relied mainly upon bribery or threats. Then an elderly woman said that she would break up the friendship— by using the power of secrets.

"What do you mean?" the mayor asked her. The schoolmaster, too, pressed for details, but the woman smiled at them and said, "Leave it to me."

This is what happened. She filled a sedan chair— the sort that is carried by two men—with rotten manure from a dung heap. On the manure she placed a pair of leather gloves. She hired a man to beat a drum and a piper to play the pipes and dressed both in scarlet uniforms. Then the procession set off for the woods where the boys were known to be hunting that day. The drummer went first, then the sedan chair and two carriers, next the piper, and finally a dancing bear that could play the tambourine with a marvelously gentle touch. The mayor and the schoolmaster watched nervously what they had set in motion, for they had never seen the like of it.

Neither had the boys. They guessed that in the chair, behind those curtains, there must be a princess on her way to somewhere—although they could not explain the drummer or the piper, not to mention the bear.

Coming closer, they smelled a bad smell.

"Can we look?" asked the schoolmaster's son.

"Look all you want," said the old woman.

They were amazed to find a pile of dung inside the chair, with a pair of gloves on top.

"What's going on?" asked the son of the mayor.

"Something too important to tell aloud," said the old woman. "It's a secret thing. Although . . . Aren't you the mayor's son? Come here and I'll whisper to you."

So the boy came close, and the old woman whispered into his ear the word "laugh"—which he did. Then she said, "Pretend that you are amazed"—which he did also. The woman whispered more noises into the boy's ear, but actually she said nothing that made sense. Then she followed the procession.

As soon as the whole mad circus was out of sight, the schoolmaster's son asked his friend what the old woman had told him.

"She told me nothing," was the reply.

"Of course she told you something; I saw you laugh. Then you were amazed. What's it all about, the dancing bear, the pipers?"

"Well . . ."

"I saw you! You were amazed."

"Yes, but she didn't tell me anything."

"I've never known you to laugh at nothing, be amazed at nothing." The schoolmaster's son paused to get at the truth of the matter. "She told you because you're the mayor's son; are you denying that?"

"No, but . . ."

"And you won't tell me because I'm not the mayor's son; is that it? You mean to keep the secret to yourself."

"There is no secret!"

Thus began the argument, which soon roared like a forest fire. One was "a lying snob," the other "a worthless idiot." Each showed a side of himself not seen by the other before. Indeed, for a time it seemed as though they might use the violence they normally reserved for partridges and wild boars, but they stopped short of shooting each other and went home early that day.

The friendship between the son of the mayor and the schoolmaster's son was never the same again; although whether they grew up to become a politician and a lawyer is not known.

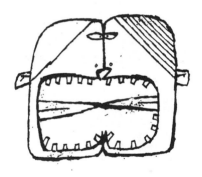

There are many stories about clever peasants
and their so-called "betters." This one tells how
a grand old duke earned his nickname.

DUKE RICHARD

THERE WAS a grand old duke who owned every field
for miles around, and a rich old duke was he. However,
apart from a bad temper, wealth was the only thing he
had, for he had no manners, no friends, no sense of
humor, and no good word to say about anybody. His
name was Richard, but no one ever called him that.
They called him . . . Well, you shall hear what they
called him.

One day, as the Grand Old Duke was riding across
his land, he spied a country girl with a jug in her hands.
Thinking that there might be cider in the jug, or at least
some refreshing drink, Duke Richard spoke to her
sternly.

"You there, girl! What have you got in that clay pot
to offer to your betters?"

"Porridge, sir," the girl replied truthfully. She was taking the porridge to her father across the fields.

"Sticky cold porridge! I can think of nothing worse!"

"I can easily heat it up," said the girl. "This is a magic jug." And so saying, she placed the jug on the stump of a tree and ran around it several times.

Then she removed the lid and showed the contents to the duke. To his amazement, a cloud of steam enveloped his nose. The porridge was practically boiling.

"It heated *itself*?"

"You saw what happened, sir."

"Without a fire?"

"All I did was set the jug on the stump of a tree, run around and around, and the porridge is hot."

Now here's a fine thing! thought Duke Richard, who was much impressed. He had heard of such miraculous pots, of course, but until this moment he had always thought them to be the silly invention of storytellers.

How could he get this jug of jugs for himself?

"If you want to give me a present of that jug, my girl," he said, "I shall be happy to accept it."

"But I'm very fond of my jug, sir," came the bold reply.

"A good thrashing with my riding whip might make you less fond of it!"

"Then I might drop the jug, sir, and it might hit a stone and break into lots of little bits. Why don't I sell it to you for five gold pieces?"

Cheap at the price, thought the duke as he loosened the strings of his purse. Already a plan had formed in his head: he would invite some important people to lunch and serve them soft-boiled eggs all cooked in the magic pot. How his guests would stare, and how they would envy him! He'd be the talk of the countryside.

Well, the pot was purchased, the invitations were sent out, and the guests duly arrived. Duke Richard set the magic jug on a tree stump, filled it with water and some eggs, and told his servant to run around it.

"Be ready to be amazed," he warned his guests.

The good servant ran as well as he was able, but the water did not boil. The duke then set his page to run also, but he made no difference, and neither did the cook. *Maybe the owner of the jug has to run, too!* thought the duke. Into the circle of runners he went—

servant, page boy, cook, and duke. They ran until they were red in the face, but the water didn't warm, the eggs didn't boil, and the people watching laughed until their legs went weak.

"Poor old Duke Rich-and-Poor," they said. "He's rich in money, but poor in everything else—especially brains!"

And from that time on, until the end of the old man's days, whenever tongues did their talking, they spoke of Duke Rich-and-Poor.

It is difficult to feel sorry for thieves, who usually don't care two hoots about the pain and trouble they cause. You might have some sympathy, however, for the fellow who was caught stealing onions.

CONSEQUENCES

TWO CONSTABLES brought an onion thief before the magistrate, who spoke to him gravely in a deep voice. "Someone else grew these onions, and yet you stole them. Another person watered them, cared for them, harvested them, stored them, and got them ready for market—only to find them stolen. By you. You."

The thief stood there, looking at his feet, humbly awaiting his sentence. It duly came.

"You will pay a fine of one hundred rupees, or receive one hundred lashes with the whip, or eat a hundred onions at one sitting. You may choose your punishment."

The thief replied at once, "I choose to eat the onions."

But they were not mild onions. After eating a dozen or so, our thief shook his head, blinked the tears from his running eyes, and cried out, "My mouth is burning; my throat is raw. I'll have to take the lashes!"

So they started with the whip. Six or seven strokes were quite enough for our poor thief, who soon began to shriek at the top of his voice, "Stop it, I beg you! This cannot go on. May heaven help me. It breaks my heart, but I'll pay; I'll pay the hundred rupees!"

And so it was that the onion thief sampled all three punishments, rather than only one.

THE WISDOM OF
SOLOMON

TWO WOMEN came before King Solomon and told him of the grievous dispute they were having, which concerned a baby.

One of them said, "My lord King, this woman and I live in the same house. A baby was born to me not long ago, and she also had a baby a few days later. They were boys. During the night, this woman's son died because she lay on him, so she gave her baby to me while I slept and took mine. When I got up to nurse my son, he was dead! Then I looked closely at him in the morning light, and he was not the child I gave birth to."

The other woman said, "No, the dead one is yours, and you are making up lies to get mine!"

In this way, they argued bitterly before Solomon.

The king said, "Bring me a sword." So they brought a sword for the king. He then gave an order: "Cut the living child in two and give half to one woman and half to the other."

One woman said, "Yes, it shall be neither mine nor yours. Divide it."

The other cried out from the depths of her sorrow and pain, "Ah, mercy, my lord, let her have my baby — only I beg you do not kill him."

Solomon sent the sword away and gave his ruling. "This is the mother, the one who would have spared the child from the sword. Give her the baby."

INTELLIGENCE
MEETS LUCK

ONE DAY Luck saw Intelligence sitting on a garden seat.

"Would you like to shove along and make room for me, there?" Luck said lightly. In the warm weather, he fancied a rest, you see. He didn't know that Intelligence was a bit jealous of him. Luck was a cheerful sort, not a bit weighed down by heavy thoughts.

"Why should I make room for you?" said Intelligence. "You think you're the better man, is that it?"

"Why, the better man is he who can do most," answered Luck, full of mischief. "Do you see that peasant boy plowing in that field? We'll go into his head, you and me, and see how he gets on. If you make him more successful than I do, well, so be it. I'll call you the better man and bow to you in the street. You go first."

Intelligence agreed, and at once entered the plowboy's head. It wasn't long before the boy began to think thoughts that, until now, he'd never had before. At dinner that night, he amazed his family by announcing that he was giving up plowing fields. "It's not the sort of life for me," he said. "I'm going up to the castle to get a job working in the gardens."

So he did. And what is more, he soon came to the notice of the king's head gardener, for he had the knack of knowing which plants to grow where, and he knew when to plant them. The whole place looked as pretty as a picture, so that even the king sent his personal congratulations to all his staff.

Never have I seen anyone with such green fingers, the head gardener said to himself. *That boy can think! I'll give him a cottage in the castle grounds in case he gets a job somewhere else.*

All was going very well for our plowboy, until one day, he saw the king's only daughter.

Of course, he knew that he ought not to fall in love with her. Intelligence told him so; but she was as lovely as a lake in moonlight. He knew it was madness to spy on her, that she already had a boyfriend, that she would never look twice at a peasant whose bare hands worked the soil. And he knew that the king guarded his daughter so carefully that unwelcome suitors usually lost their heads. Intelligence told him so.

But knowing didn't matter. He planted night-scented flowers beneath her window so that she would be drawn to her balcony in the evenings when he spied on her—his lovely princess. On the day of her marriage to a prince from some foreign country, a fit of madness came over the plowboy, and he danced on the bed of night-scented flowers, ruining it completely.

Of course he knew, none more so, that he should not drink; but drink he did, and drunk he became, so that he ran about the castle saying things about the royal princess that should never have been said, even had they been true, which they were not.

"Hang him," said the king when he heard. "Hang him by the neck and hang him high."

And so the plowboy was taken in an unsprung wagon to the gallows at the crossroads beyond the castle walls. The awful rope swayed ever so slightly as it dangled down, wanting only a neck in the noose.

Luck was there, in the front row of spectators.

"Here's a fine pickle!" he whispered to Intelligence. "The plowboy has done so well with you in his head that he's soon to swing from a rope! Make way, and let me take your place."

Once Luck appeared in the picture, a brighter end to the story was inevitable. The hanging rope had been nearly gnawed through by a hungry rat and easily broke under the weight of the plowboy. The prisoner fell through a trapdoor into the wagon waiting to take him to the cemetery, but of course he headed at full speed for the nearest hills. There, it is said, he met up with traveling people and became a performing artist in a circus; although that is a story for another time.

Now you know why Intelligence will always give a little bow to Luck, although he tries to avoid that trickster if he can.

The tellers of stories know that
the best treasure is buried treasure.

RICHES IN THE SOIL

IN DAYS GONE BY, there were three brothers who found buried treasure in an unexpected way. . . .

Now, the three brothers were idle fellows who had never done a decent day's work in their lives. They had no need to, or so they said, for their father was a rich farmer and the owner of four large fields. Upon the old man's death, the land would surely come to them, along with all the money that he'd worked so hard for. So it was a case of "eat, drink, and be merry" for the three loafers.

Then one day the old farmer called for his sons to stand by his bedside. There was something he wanted to say.

"I am leaving the land to all three of you. You may choose to sell it and divide the money, but be aware that I have buried most of my treasure in the first field."

Then he said good-bye and waved them away, for he knew he had the illness that would kill him soon.

Shortly after his death, his sons began to dig in what they thought was the first field. Naturally enough, they were anxious to get their hands on the treasure. They dug all day for many a day, and they dug deep, but not a thing did they find of any value.

"We've been digging in the wrong place," one of them said eventually. "Maybe one of the others is the first field. We should have asked him!"

Before starting on the second field, however, they had the good sense to sow some seed in the one they'd just dug. A good crop would bring in some money, at least.

They found no treasure in the second field, either, in spite of all their labors. Unfortunately, it wasn't the kind of work that they could pay someone else to do — the someone else might make off with the treasure! Once again they sowed corn, hoping to profit a little from the sweat of their brows and their aching backs.

Then they dug up and planted the third field and the fourth. It was clear to them now that they had missed the treasure—perhaps through bad luck or because their father had been confused in his last days.

They decided to go over the fields again, digging deeper this time. Meanwhile, they harvested their corn and took it to the marketplace. The brothers were pleasantly surprised by how much they made from selling it.

They dug again and planted again. They got used to hard labor. They were proud of the crops they grew. As the seasons went by, they came to cherish the land they owned. They were farmers.

These were the riches found by the brothers in the soil, left to them by their father's hand.

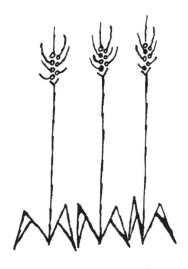

HISTORY AND SWIMMING

A HISTORY PROFESSOR once paid a ferryman to take him across a river in a boat. The river was fast-flowing after recent floods, but the historian was in a hurry and the ferryman was greedy. He took the money and began to row.

"Have you ever studied history, my good fellow?" the professor asked his companion.

"No," replied the ferryman, with one eye on the choppy water.

"More's the pity! The study of history helps us to make sense of what is happening in the world."

"Aye, you might be right," said the ferryman.

"Of course I'm right. I could quote a hundred examples. Why, the first part of your life has been wasted if you don't know any history!"

A log came swirling toward them out of the churning white water, and there was a thud somewhere near the bow of the boat, followed by a sharp crack.

"Can you swim?" asked the ferryman, knee-deep in water.

"Swim? I never had time to learn how to swim!"

"Then the second part of your life is wasted, my friend, for I can't save the two of us."

Your Collector of Stories does not believe in ghosts, but some people do. This story is for them.

A SMALL VOICE RISING

IN THE NORTHEAST of Ireland, there once was a child who died without a name.

No one knows how the child died or why it had no name. He or she was buried not far from the sea, near a place called the Gobbin Shore. And before long, the people of the area began to speak in whispers about a voice that was heard in the night, a child's voice, rising as if in lamentation above the sounds of wind and tide. Fishermen, coming home in their boats, claimed to see a tiny light moving along the stony shore between the ocean and the cliffs. The child walked with a candle in its hand, people said—and the child spoke. What did it say? At first no one would venture close enough to find out.

Then William Mann set out one night for the Gobbin Shore. He had the usual fears of ordinary people, but it was his way to face up to those fears and master them: he was a strong man in his mind.

There was no easy landing place on the Gobbin Shore, so he ran his punt in with the tide and stepped out onto the shingle. Before long he saw a flickering light and heard the sound of someone speaking. "That's a wee one's voice, right enough," he muttered to himself.

Presently he came to where a waiflike figure sat on the rocks, holding a lit candle. The night wind tugged at the candle's flame but could not put it out.

"I have no name," the small voice seemed to say.

William Mann came closer. "What are you trying to tell me?" he said.

"I have no name. I am a child without a name."

"Sure that'll never do; everybody has to have a name," said Mann. "If you're a boy, I gladly give you my own name, William, and if you're a girl, I give you my wife's name, Maud. So I'll go away now. And you go away, too, and content yourself, because now you do have a name."

The lit candle was never seen again on that stretch of the Gobbin Shore, nor did anyone hear the small voice rising of the child called William or Maud.

Don't expect gratitude to last, for often it
melts away like footprints in the snow.

GET ME DOWN!

A COUNTRY FELLOW set off one day to cut some
winter firewood in the forest. He climbed a mighty tree,
lopping off a branch here and another one there, until
he got near the top, looked down, and felt his poor heart
lurch with panic, for he'd cut off the very branches he
would need to get down again! He was stuck eighty feet
up in the air.

The first thing he did was shout for help, but that
was no use. The only creatures near him wore feathers.
At last he lifted up his eyes to the heavens and spoke
humbly to Allah.

"Only get me out of the trouble I'm in, and the best
of what I have shall be yours! O Allah, even the value of
my house, I dedicate to you!"

At the finish of the prayer, our man slipped down
the tree quite a few feet. Mind you, he still couldn't
bear to look down, but he tried another prayer.

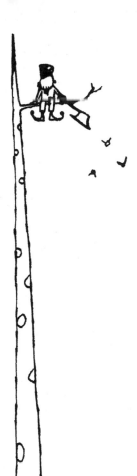

"Allah, bring me down safely and I shall worship you and dedicate to you the full value of my finest bull!"

There came another slip and slide, and our man found himself halfway down the tree. There was a fair drop left, of course, more than enough to reduce a man to a bag of broken bones.

"O Allah, who sees all, let me come safely down the tree and you shall have the full price of my bearded goat; I mean the very one my neighbor wants so much!"

Slithering and sliding, the adventurer managed to reach a foothold not so far from the ground. "Allah, I shall dedicate a hen to you, my best layer, that fat speckled one, if you get me down without a fall!"

With a little more maneuvering, and after promising Allah a basket of eggs, he came safely to firm ground. Now the woodcutter looked up into the tree and felt very pleased with himself. "O Allah," he said, "I climbed up the tree by myself and I climbed back down by myself. I'm sure you don't want to be bothered with my little problems."

So saying, he gathered up his wood and went home.

THE VERY
EXPENSIVE CAT

IN FORMER TIMES, there was a woman who found, like many before her, that life is full of difficulties. She promised in her prayers that if her problems were solved, she would sell her house and give the money to the poor.

I won't give details about the problems she had, except to say that they were to do with her health. Neither shall I describe her house, except to note that many people in the area had been after it for years. They loved its views, its split-level gardens, and its closeness to the ever-changing sea.

A year went by. All the worries that had clouded the woman's thoughts were gone, and she no longer mentioned them in her prayers. She was as well as she had ever been, and yet she could not forget the oath she'd made: money for peace of mind. Must she now sell her house and give the proceeds to the poor?

Yes. Although the move would bring her heartache, an agreement had been made—a contract—and she must honor it by selling her property. But, of course, she knew its value and could not bear the thought of giving up all that money. Such a house might fetch twelve thousand golden guineas!

So she thought of a way out. The house was put on the market for a single golden guinea. Just one. Included with the house, however, was a cat. The person who bought the house for a guinea was obliged to buy the cat, too, and the price of the cat was ten thousand golden guineas. When the house was sold after a few weeks, the woman gave one golden guinea to the poor and kept ten thousand for herself.

THE SHADOW OF
THE MULE

ONE DAY a merchant hired a mule to bring his goods into town. He also took along the owner of the beast to keep it under control.

On the way home, in the heat of the day, they stopped to rest, and the merchant wanted to lie down in the mule's shadow. But the owner, who also wanted to be out of the sun, wouldn't let him do that.

"From me you hired only the mule," he said. "There was no mention of its shadow."

"I never heard such garbage," replied the merchant. "I hired the whole animal for the entire day, and that includes its shadow!"

"Not so. You only paid for the use of my mule."

"Exactly. I want to use its shadow."

"It's mine! You hired the mule's labor. The shadow belongs to me."

"Do you expect to get away with this cheap trick?"

"Do you expect to use my mule as a parasol? For nothing?"

The argument proceeded quickly from words to blows, which made them hotter still. And all the while, the mule went on its way and came back home without them—along with its shadow.

DOCTOR JACK POWERS

IN AN OLD sea port in northern Europe, a man set out to walk home from a tavern. I'll give him the name of Jack Powers. He was looking forward to a supper of trout served up with parsley, warm bread, and a light white wine, but he failed to reach his house that night. A gang of sailors pounced on him, tied him up, and carried him away to serve on a ship of the king's navy.

That's how they solved their recruitment problem in those days.

So Jack Powers was brought before the governor, who asked him if there was a good reason why he should not be a willing sailor for seven good years and defend his country from its enemies.

Our man Jack had to think quickly. *Now I'm in for it,* he said to himself. *Seven long years of scrubbing the deck of a ship! Of dodging French or Spanish cannon-balls. Of putting up sails and hauling down sails in the worst of gales.* He blurted out the first thing that came into his head. "But I'm a doctor," he said.

The governor did not believe him, for he had in his head an idea of what a doctor should look like, and Jack Powers didn't match up. Nevertheless, he had to be careful. . . . You can bop almost anyone on the head, carry him off to sea against his will, and his absence will never be noticed by anyone whose opinion matters; but a doctor? A doctor might be missed by some important people.

"Put him in jail for the night, and in the morning we'll give him a test."

When the morning came, Jack found himself ushered into a great hall, where a small crowd of sick people had assembled to wait for him.

"I'll wait outside," smiled the governor. "If you're a doctor, they'll know it. If you're not . . . Well, they'll know that too." Saying which, he left the room.

In all his life, our man Jack had never set a bone, straightened a corpse, or wiped a fevered brow. If the truth be known, the mere sight of blood made him feel strangely weak, especially his own. Now here he was, in a room full of sick people clamoring to be cured.

Oh, dear me! With all the authority he could muster, Jack raised his arms to calm these folk down.

"I have to say to you, ladies and gentlemen, this is not going to be easy for you or for me."

"We've been told you are a great physician," went up the cry.

"Look, there's only one way I can help you, and here it is," said Jack, who had noticed a fine log fire burning at one end of the room. "I'm going to pick out the sickest person and burn him or her in that fire over there. Ashes to ashes. It's hard—I know it is, but that can't be helped. Life itself is hard! The rest of you will then benefit enormously from drinking a medicine made from the ashes of the deceased. You're going to feel so much better, believe me. I have seen this happen many times; it is the method that has made me famous."

People who are not used to speaking in public often find that they have a knack for it, if only they can get over their nerves. And so it was with Jack Powers. After a minute or two, he spoke like the greatest authority on health there has ever been. His audience was delighted to hear the good news of a cure, but who was the sickest person? Who was to be sacrificed for the common good, ashes to ashes? When the famous doctor pointed to an old fellow leaning on a stick, the same man straightened up, said he felt fine, and made for the door with a spring in his step. After a glance at the hot fire, several others followed his example, and soon there was a line at the door to get out.

The governor, seeing a woman hobble past in the corridor, asked how she was feeling. "Never better! That's some doctor you got for us back there!" Then she hurried away with a most curious expression on her face, crying, "Ashes to ashes!" Every person spoken to by the governor said they felt better than before. Thus Jack proved his Powers, was set at liberty, and no doubt some other unwilling soul was picked on as he walked home from the inn.

We can't all have brave hearts and be great heroes.
Your Collector of Stories suggests that most of us
have a bit of the coward in us—like the famous
Irish giant, Finn MacCool.

THE BIG BABY

FINN LIVED in that part of northeast Ireland that is
very close to Scotland. If you ever get that far, be sure to
visit the Giant's Causeway, built by Finn long ago. It's
sometimes called the eighth wonder of the world.

Now, there was a Scottish giant, too. His name was
Balfor, and he and Finn used to shout across the sea at
each other. One stood in Ireland and one stood in
Scotland, and some of the things they shouted weren't
very polite.

One day Balfor took it into his head to go over
to Ireland and give Finn MacCool a good thrashing.
Finn, standing on the shore, could see him wading
across the sea with a pine tree in his hand, shouting,
"Finn MacCool, Finn MacCool, you'll soon be Finn

MacWarm. I'm coming to get you! Yoo-hoo, Finn MacVeryhot!"

Finn ran away home to his house in the Glens of Antrim. "Balfor's coming to get me," he said to his wife, Eileen. "Where can I hide? Quick!"

"Where's the sense in hiding?" said Eileen. "Surely he'll only wait until you come back. Don't be such a big baby."

"What'll I do, then?" wailed Finn, hearing the thud of distant footsteps. Balfor was coming!

The word "baby" gave Eileen a good idea. She whisked their own baby out of its cradle, shoved the dear little thing under the sink, and told Finn to get into the cradle instead. Then she covered him with a blanket, stuck a pacifier in his mouth, and warned him to lie still and say nothing.

There were some pancakes baking on the fire. Eileen hid a big metal spoon in one of the pancakes, just as a mighty Scottish foot flattened her front door.

"Finn MacCool!" roared Balfor.

"That's no way to come into anybody's house," said Eileen. "My husband will be back soon. Try one of my pancakes while you're waiting for him."

She gave him the pancake with the spoon in it, and the roar from Balfor nearly lifted the roof. He spat out at least two teeth and wiped the tears from his eyes.

"Och, gimme that," said Eileen. "What sort of soft jaws have you got? My baby loves them pancakes, and he hasn't even got all his teeth yet." So saying, she offered the pancake to Finn, who ate it in one bite now that there was no spoon in it.

Hmm, thought Balfor. *That's a strong baby. A big baby.* Leaning over the cradle for a look, he found his nose suddenly grabbed, pulled, and twisted until it went numb, and more tears came to his eyes. In fact, Balfor rushed to look in a mirror to be sure his nose was still on his face.

"That's one terrible strong baby you have there," he said.

"His dad will be back soon. He's moving a mountain for the local people—it was a wee bit close to the town."

"A mountain? How big a mountain?"

"Oh, as big as you like," said Eileen. "As high as the clouds, anyway. What did you want him for?"

"Eh . . ." Balfor glanced once more at the baby in the cradle and tried to imagine its dad. Might Finn MacCool be more of a handful than he thought? "It doesn't matter. I have to go now."

Which he did. Balfor never came back to Ireland, and you can be sure that Finn, being Finn, never went looking for him.

A FREE SPIRIT

AN EMPEROR of eastern lands had a great love of good music. There was in his court a fine singer of traditional songs, who went by the name of Isak. After one particular evening of entertainment, the emperor was moved to say, "Isak, you are the best of singers—there can be no better voice in my kingdom."

"Thank you, my lord," said Isak. "I don't know how many singers might be better than I, but there is certainly one—my teacher, Alsa Shad."

"You must take me to him! I won't believe he's your equal until I hear him sing."

Isak began to frown. He was thinking that music teachers tend to be an eccentric lot, and Alsa Shad was more eccentric than most.

"He might not sing for Your Majesty," replied Isak. "I'm not at all sure how he would feel about singing for the emperor himself. It would be best if you disguise yourself when we go to visit."

133

"Agreed," cried the emperor, who was already looking forward to the adventure.

Thus it happened that Isak and his servant went to see his old teacher, who had no idea that the servant was none other than his emperor. They chatted pleasantly about old times, but Alsa Shad refused to sing.

"No, not now," he said. "It doesn't feel like a singing sort of day. Another time, perhaps."

It was more or less the reply that Isak had expected, and he met it with a plan. Now he began to sing himself, and the song he sang was an old song, one of Alsa Shad's favorites. Here and there he got the phrasing wrong or allowed his voice to miss a note, until Alsa Shad shook his head impatiently, for he could not bear to hear the beloved song sung badly.

"What am I hearing! The fancy life you lead is spoiling you, Isak—where is your attention to detail? The high notes should be sweet and round. Listen!"

And he sang.

On the way home, the emperor admitted to Isak that he had never heard anyone with the power, the passion, and the skill of Alsa Shad.

"How is it that he sings even better than you, Isak?"

"I'm not sure, Sire. Perhaps it's because I perform mainly to please others—on command, as it were. But my teacher, Alsa Shad, sings when the spirit moves him. He is a free man who sings for the love of music and to please himself."

IS IT FAIR?

MANY YEARS AGO, when wolves ran wild in the hills of China, a scholarly man called Wan Li walked home from town. He had a donkey with him to carry his books and groceries.

It was a fine summer evening, and from across the valley he could hear the horns of a hunting party sounding out. And then, without the least hint of a warning, a wolf rushed from the cover of some bushes and stood before him in the lane.

"You must hide me," cried the wolf. "A warlord is after me with hunting dogs and arrows. I can tell that you are a man of peace—will you let a fellow creature die?"

"But . . . where can I hide you?" asked Wan Li, much taken aback.

"In one of the baskets on your donkey. Quick, they'll soon be here! Think how you'll feel if you see me torn apart. After all, I, too, am of this earth."

So Wan Li removed the books from a basket, and the wolf jumped in. As the horses of the hunt came sweeping by in a swirl of sound and dust, no one gave a second glance at the scholar with the slow old donkey.

And so the wolf was saved. It jumped out from the basket with an unpleasant glint in its eye.

"Now that the danger is past," the wolf said to the scholar, "I'm afraid I'm going to have to eat you."

"But I saved your life!" cried Wan Li.

"And what was the point of saving my life if now you let me die of starvation? No. I'm tired and hungry after the chase. Eat you I must."

"This cannot be fair," said the scholar nervously, for the creature seemed to be serious about eating him. "Let us walk along this path—with the donkey between us—and ask the opinion of those we meet. If three opinions go against me, I shall agree to be eaten."

"As you wish," said the wolf, knowing full well that the old fellow could never run fast enough to escape from him.

They came to a walnut tree and asked it whether the wolf was entitled to eat the scholar.

"The people around here take away the nuts I grow," the walnut tree began mournfully, "then they come back for branches to burn. I cannot escape the ax. I can't escape the saw, either, for someday they'll come and cut me down for furniture. As men have used me, let that man there be used. May the wolf eat up and enjoy!"

"One to me," said the wolf.

They came to an ox in a field and asked whether it was fair for the wolf to eat the scholar. The ox said, "My master is a farmer. For years I pulled the cart; I pulled the plow; I pulled stumps out of ditches. Everything of any use to that man came from me. Look at the fields where once there were stones and puddles of clay—all good land. My labor. Now I'm old, and still it goes on. There is no rest from the effort of making my master rich. Look at me. I tire in the sun, freeze in the wind, and my hooves rot in the rain. If the wolf is the master now, let him take good advantage. Eat away, I say!"

"Two for me, I think," grinned the wolf.

They came to an owl sitting in an oak. Once more Wan Li told his story, saying, "Surely you can see how it would be against all fairness for the wolf to eat me. One good turn deserves another."

"Not necessarily," replied the owl. "After all, a wolf is like anyone else; it must eat. But let me get the facts straight. Can it really be true, Wolf, that you hid in that basket? It's not a big basket, and you are not a small wolf. I could only believe such a thing if I saw it with my own eyes. If your story is true, show me."

"It is true," cried the wolf. "Watch this!"

In he jumped and nestled down in the basket so that there wasn't a hair of his back showing. Then the owl said quietly. "If I were you, Master Scholar, I would tie down the lid of that basket before your prisoner gets out. And take care whom you help in the future, for you've just had a lucky escape. What's fair for one need not be fair for another."

TALKING TURKEY

IN ANOTHER TIME and place, there was a king
who broke a bone in his leg and had to stay in bed for a
month. His young wife made good use of her husband's
illness by shopping every day and having parties in the
evenings.

In the morning there was a lot of cleaning up to be
done after the night before. One day it happened that a
cleaning woman noticed forty turkeys in a pen outside
the queen's bedchamber. They were fine birds, every
one as plump as could be and worth more than a penny
or two.

"O Queen of night and day," the old woman said,
"may I inquire if these birds of yours can talk?"

"Of course they can't talk," replied the queen. "No
more than I can fly."

"If you let me have them for six weeks and a day, I
will train them to talk."

The queen had never heard of such a thing, but she agreed to have the birds trained. Talking turkeys would be a novelty at one of her grand entertainments.

"Of course," the old woman went on, "I will require several hundred sacks of corn. The birds must eat."

The queen told her to go and speak to whoever dealt with that sort of thing, which she did. That very day the forty fine turkeys went home with her to her cottage at the edge of the woods. She killed one that same night and hung it up to bleed, intending to cook it for tomorrow's supper.

During the next few weeks, she ate a number of the turkeys herself. Some of them she gave to her children and her grandchildren, and one to a neighbor who had done her a favor last winter. Master Fox ran away with two or three. After a while, not one of the forty turkeys was left.

Six weeks and a day went by. The queen was more careful about how she spent her time, for the king was now able to get about with the aid of a walking stick — less shopping, not so many parties.

An old woman appeared before her, looking worried. At first the queen could not remember why she seemed familiar.

"What's the matter with you?" asked the queen. "Why are you hovering there?"

"It's the turkeys," came the reply, "the ones that used to be outside Your Majesty's bedroom. I have trained them to talk, and now they are all saying the same strange thing."

Of course. The turkeys! They had been a present from her husband. He had wanted to give her peacocks,

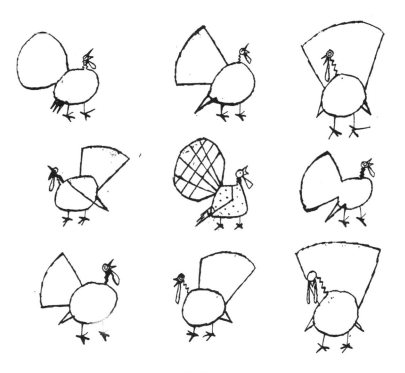

143

but she had a superstition about peacocks. They bring bad luck.

"What are the turkeys saying?" asked the queen.

"They say: 'She has a secret; our queen has a secret; we know she has a secret!' And I cannot stop them; nothing seems to change their song. I don't know what to do."

For a moment or two, the queen held herself very still. Then she said, "I never liked them. You will get rid of those birds, all of them, and on no account bring them near the palace. Do you hear what I'm saying? Dispose of them as you will."

The old woman nodded to show that she understood, then withdrew from the royal presence.

Most of us are brought up to know the difference between right and wrong. Of course, that doesn't always make us do the right thing.

ASKING PERMISSION

A MAN called Waghar once discovered how easy it is to steal. When no one was looking, he helped himself to potatoes from a field near his house. This was a lot cheaper than buying them in the usual way, and much more convenient. They were so fresh, too! Waghar had no idea who owned the potatoes, but since he knew very well that they didn't belong to him, he used to say out loud, "Field, field, may I pick some of your potatoes for my dinner tonight?" And Waghar himself answered— as if he were the field—"Of course you can, dear Waghar, you may have three or four; or perhaps even six."

Somehow this made him feel better about stealing the potatoes; it eased his conscience.

Now the man who actually owned the field of potatoes was Alvar Tomas, a man who could sniff a thief a mile away—even a crafty thief who stole a plant here and a plant there, but never two plants from the same row. So he rose early one morning, hid himself behind a hedge, and waited.

Along came Waghar, carrying a little leather bag and a short spade. "Field, field, may I have something for my dinner tonight?" he said, and then he answered, "Of course, Waghar, you may have enough potatoes to fill a small bag." He plunged his spade into the earth, and that was the moment when a rope fell about his shoulders, frightening him half to death and making him a prisoner.

Now Waghar found himself at the mercy of Alvar Tomas, who held in his hand a stout stick from the hedge. "Well, stick," he said, "how many times shall I whack this potato thief?" And Alvar Tomas himself answered—as if he were the stick—"Don't be stingy, Alvar! One or two is no good. Let him have a dozen!"

Poor old Waghar. He begged forgiveness and promised not to go near those potatoes again. He never stole another thing after that experience, because he knew it was wrong; and besides, his nerves weren't up to it.

Is there such a thing as "justice"? Your Collector of Stories believes that most of us like to think so.

TWISTING THE TRUTH

MYNA DORNAN worked as a government clerk—a notary—in a busy town. This quiet, patient woman wore out quills and candles recording the births, deaths, and marriages of her fellow citizens.

One day she was charged with falsifying a document and brought to court. An important lawyer claimed she took money to change some details on a rich man's death certificate. At first Myna Dornan thought there had been a silly misunderstanding, but the truth soon hit her: a fortune was at stake because of the dead man's will, and this was serious. She was a pawn in a game she didn't understand and might easily go to jail for accepting bribes!

The prosecuting lawyer was a bully to whom the twisting of words came as naturally as a smile. He was a smooth-talking, educated, cultivated cheat, who sold his talents to the highest bidder and whose guiding principle was to win the game by whatever means possible. He relied on his victims, being ordinary people, to be frightened in court.

Now it was Myna Dornan's turn. She faced him full square and looked him in the eye. Had she falsified a death certificate? Certainly not. Had she taken money to lie about the cause of death? No! Point by point, she refuted the arguments of her accuser. The ink was not hers, the writing was not hers, the quill was not cut like hers. And where had she spent the bribe she was supposed to have taken? Or having kept the money, where was it now? "The prosecuting lawyer is twisting my words," said Myna Dornan, "and when you twist words, you twist the truth."

Then the prosecutor, sensing that he had met his match, said to the chief magistrate, "All this talk of facts! I say let us leave the matter to God, who already knows the facts and who sees clearly. Let Him be the judge."

"Explain," said the magistrate.

"I shall put two pieces of paper into this box. On one paper I will write the word 'guilty'; the other is simply blank. Let the notary draw out one piece of paper, and we shall see what the Almighty says. This has been done before in difficult cases."

It was agreed. The two pieces of paper, carefully prepared by the prosecutor, went into the box. Myna Dornan reached in, drew one out, and without so much as a glance at it, thrust it into the flame of the nearest candle. After a spurt of yellow light, the paper crumbled into ash.

"What are you doing?" raged the prosecutor. "We need to see what was written."

"Then I beg the magistrate to look at the paper still in the box," said Myna Dornan.

They did so.

"The word 'guilty' is written here," said the chief magistrate. "Then it must follow that the other paper was blank." He nodded at the notary, signifying that she was free to go.

This was the just verdict, of course: Myna Dornan was as honest as the day is long. And yet . . . what if she had not guessed correctly that the prosecutor would write "guilty" on both pieces of paper?

Have you ever looked up at the stars at night and wondered what it's all about? Is there a Grand Plan? What is the Big Picture? Many people have claimed to know what it's all about, but not one of them has ever satisfied your Collector of Stories. Perhaps that's why I like this tale so much.

THE ELEPHANT

SOME TRAVELERS went on a journey over the mountains by elephant. One evening they lodged in a village whose inhabitants, being blind, had never seen an elephant. The people of the village were curious about the nature of the beast and sent some of their elders to investigate.

The first elder, exploring with his hands, came across the elephant's ear and declared that the animal reminded him of nothing so much as a fan for cooling oneself in hot weather. A second elder, after feeling a leg, thought the elephant was almost certainly a thing with pillars. Then the third elder, holding the trunk, suggested that one should think of the beast as a kind of waterspout. The fourth elder, speaking from a perch on the elephant's back, announced that he was sitting on what could only be described as a seat for kings—a veritable throne.

The four elders reported their experiences to the other villagers, but as to what a real elephant actually looked like, everyone remained very much in the dark.

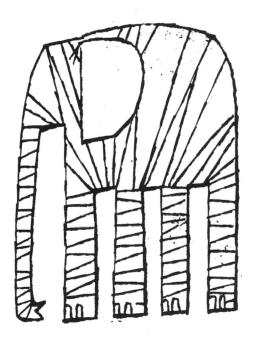

A LESSON WORTH LEARNING

IN A TIME before this, there lived a man who made a promise to his wife but didn't keep it. He said that he would bring home a length of cloth from the market, and when he came home empty-handed, his wife called him a worthless husband.

"How am I to make clothes for us all?" she said. "How can I make clothes if I have no cloth?"

"Tomorrow," grunted the man, whose name was Matthau. "I will bring you cloth tomorrow."

But Matthau had spent all his money on winter feed for his animals, so when tomorrow came, he rose early and set out to do something he had never done before. He armed himself with stones, hid behind a tree, and waited. While he waited, he rubbed his face with mud to disguise his features. Before long a stranger came by, carrying a bundle of cloth. Matthau jumped out and hurled a stone into his ribs. Another stone caused the poor fellow to sink to his knees.

"What do you want from me?" the wounded man cried out.

"Your bundle of cloth," said Matthau, letting loose another stone.

"Take the cloth! I'll give it to you, only drop your stones and leave me alone."

"You'll give it to me?" shouted Matthau, who was angry at himself for what he was doing. "You think I'm some kind of beggar? A thief is bad enough, but a beggar I will never be!"

Another stone cut the stranger, who said, "What kind of beast are you? I'm in pain and defenseless, and still you hurt me." Then he ran for his life as best he could.

When Matthau came home that day, his wife could not hide her delight, for there was more cloth—and of a better quality—than she could have hoped for.

"Where did you get it?"

"I got it. Don't ask."

"I don't care where you got it," said his wife. "We have as much need of it as anyone else."

Some months went by. The summer had come and almost gone when Matthau went to buy a sack of lentils at the market. While going from stall to stall, he felt a hand fall gently on his shoulder and, turning, found himself face-to-face with the very man whom he'd robbed some months before.

"So what are you buying, friend?"

"Lentils," said Matthau.

"You mustn't buy them here," said the stranger. "Come with me. I have lentils."

"But . . ."

"This way; my house is quite near."

Matthau saw that he must go, for the marketplace was full of the man's companions, some armed with swords and even rifles. After a short walk, they came to a lime-washed house, where the stranger called for a meal to be prepared. With the twilight approaching, Matthau was shown to a cool room with fresh bedding. In the morning he ate oat flakes topped with pale honey, and all the while he kept wondering why the stranger was showing such kindness to him—especially when it was time to leave, and he saw that the saddlebags of his donkey were full of lentils.

"How much do I owe you for the lentils?" Matthau said to his host, who shook his head.

"Nothing. I am giving them to you."

Then Matthau set off for home. But after a few steps, he stopped, turned, and said, "You recognize me, don't you? You know what I did."

"I remember."

Overcome with a burning shame, Matthau cried out, "How can I accept these lentils when we both know how I robbed you? I won't take them!"

The stranger said, "I don't know who you are or what you may become, but I have been showing you how a man ought to behave toward other people. It's a lesson worth learning—and you certainly need teaching."

In this way, Matthau went home with his saddle-bags full of lentils and a heart brimming with remorse.

Your Collector of Stories, an occasional fisherman, pleads guilty. He enjoys an activity that involves the death of another creature.

SAYING GRACE

A HUNTER who loved to stalk large cats and shoot them dead once came face-to-face with a lion and found that his gun would not fire.

What should he do? To run seemed worse than useless—with two bounds through the savanna grass, the lion would surely have him. And it was too late to hide. Already the black-and-yellow eyes were watching him. In those dreadful seconds, the hunter knew what it felt like to stand cornered, defenseless, alone: the hunted one.

Something he'd read came to mind: that he should pretend to be dead. If the animal had eaten recently, it might leave him alone. So the hunter fell to his knees, placed his forehead on the ground, and covered his head with his hands.

After some moments of tremendous suspense, he risked a glance at the lion. To his amazement, the creature also seemed to be kneeling there, with its great head resting on its paws. Then it spoke!

"I've no idea what you're doing," said the lion, "but I'm saying grace."

As is often the way, the hunter woke up before the worst would happen, for he had dreamed the whole thing. Lying there in the cold damp of his own sweat, he wondered for the first time about the rights and wrongs of shooting an animal dead just for the fun of it.

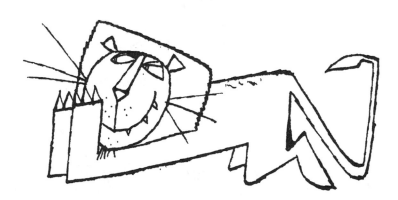

THE SOUP STONE

A RUSSIAN SOLDIER came home on leave one time. He'd traveled many a mile and still had more to go when he chanced on a cottage with a candle in the window and smoke escaping from the chimney.

"My good lady," he said to the owner, "could a man in uniform come in and rest for a while?"

"No harm, I suppose," said the woman, widening the door for him to pass. She gave the soldier a bench seat near the fire and a hand-sewn cushion for comfort, but warned him, "I've got no food, mind you. I haven't eaten myself since yesterday morning."

In actual fact the woman had plenty of meat and vegetables, even fruit. She just didn't want to share them with a lean and hungry stranger whom she'd never seen before and would never see again.

"Not to worry," said the soldier, producing a stone from his bag, "this will make a grand pot of soup for the both of us."

"That's only a sharpening stone for a razor or a knife," said the woman.

"It's a soup stone. The army gives one of these to us soldiers before we go on a march. You're supposed to hand it in, but"—he winked at her—"I kept mine. If you kindly fetch me a pot, I'll show you how it works."

A pot was produced soon enough, into which the soldier placed his stone and covered it with water. Then he hung the pot over the fire. "There!" he said. "It will soon be boiling. At this stage I usually add a pinch of salt."

"I can let you have some salt," said the woman. And she did.

As soon as the mixture began to boil, the soldier stirred it with a spoon. Then he tasted it. "Very fine! The stone is doing its work. Mind you, a handful of leeks or whatever would make it rather special for us."

"I might have some barley and some split peas," said the woman.

"Just the job," agreed the soldier.

At the next tasting, he said that the mixture wanted only a touch of stock to make it perfect.

"There's some goose fat at the back of the larder," said the woman.

"The very thing!" agreed the soldier.

It wasn't long before they both sat down to a bowl of tasty broth with a crumbly bread made from wheat and buttermilk.

"That was a grand meal," said the woman. "I never knew the army had a thing as good as a soup stone."

The soldier smiled and thanked her kindly for the use of her pot.

Your Collector of Stories can't admit to actually liking this old European tale. Mass murder must be counted among the most horrible deeds of human nature. The story ends on a note of decency, though, and has a certain fascination. . . .

EXPERIENCE

LONG AGO, in another country, the young folk decided to get rid of people over a certain age. They no longer wanted the wisdom or the advice of the old folk, for they believed themselves to be every bit as clever. "You've lived your lives," they said to the old folk. "You've had your day. It's our turn now." Anyone who was old was made to feel like a nuisance and a burden on the rest of society.

Unfortunately, the king of that place was also a young man, surrounded by young advisers, so it was no great surprise when a law was passed declaring that old people should be killed. And that is what happened. Out from their brick barracks beneath the city walls marched the young soldiers with their swords. Before long there was no one in the land with a gray hair on his or her head.

One young woman could not bear to surrender her father to the soldiers. She hid him under the house, where he slept on a pile of old sacks. Twice a day she brought the old man food, and there he lived in a cellar, scarcely better off than a rat, for more than two years. The woman never told anyone that her father was alive down there, for she feared that they would kill him— and her, too.

In the country at large, things went well for a while. The young people brought in the harvest as usual— there was an abundance of potatoes and corn, of apples and grapes. The winter was cold, though, and a period of wicked frost destroyed the seed potatoes that should have been next year's crop. They hadn't been stored properly.

Still, they had plenty of corn. . . .

There was plenty of corn, but the following summer was so dry that not a drop of rain fell for months. The crops withered in the fields. The harvest produced less than half the grain the young ones needed. By midwinter there was something in the air so awful that they dared not speak its name: famine.

One night in the cellar, the old man looked carefully at the meal his daughter had brought him. It consisted of watered-down milk and a tiny round cake made from flour and egg white. The cakes had been getting smaller for some time now.

"Tell me what's happening, child," he said.

"There's no flour," she told him. "No flour, no bread."

"Use my money! You know it's inside the fiddle, on the back of the door."

"Money wouldn't make any difference, Father; there's no food. Nobody knows what to do. We're even eating next year's seed corn—the seed we should be keeping for sowing the fields in spring."

"Are there no seed potatoes?"

"A frost got them; they went mushy and black. And all the animals are dying. You could play a tune on the ribs of our poor goat."

The old man was silent for a while. Then, as his daughter got up to go, he said, "Elise, when you throw a fistful of flour into the mix, add the same amount of sawdust."

"Sawdust? There's no goodness in sawdust, Father."

"I know, but at least your stomach thinks it's had food. Sawdust from birchwood is the best. It's what we used to do in hard times. The mix will go further and your system has something to work on."

"Good night, Father."

Later that day, toward dusk, the old man put on a hooded cloak and sneaked out of the house. Walking toward the city, he soon saw for himself how times had changed—no children played in the dusty roads, no dogs came yapping around his legs, and such people as there were went about their business with slow steps, as if they wore boots of lead instead of leather on their feet.

He read a message pinned to the city gate:

THIS PROCLAMATION IS GIVEN

BY HIS NOBLE MAJESTY THE KING.

CITIZENS, WE LIVE IN HARD TIMES, HARDER THAN

ANYONE CAN REMEMBER. OWING TO CROP FAILURE,

ALL FOOD WILL BE RATIONED.

ANYONE WHO CAN HELP IN THIS SITUATION

MAY SPEAK FREELY AND WILL BE WELL REWARDED.

THE HOARDING OF FOOD WILL BE PUNISHED BY DEATH.

Then the old man returned to his daughter, who was angry to find that he had been out of the house. Brushing aside her protests, he spoke to her urgently: "Tomorrow you will go to the city and ask to see the advisers of the king, and you will tell them to plow up the roads."

"The roads, Father?"

"The roads, yes. And also make them strip the roofs. Come, let me explain my idea to you—and then you can explain it to them!"

So Elise went to see the king's advisers in the morning and told them what her father had said. They were young men, and they winked and smiled when they saw her. At the mention of plowing up the roads, one of the advisers laughed, and she fixed him with a stare.

"Look in the mirror if you want a laugh; you can hardly grow a mustache! When people carry grain to the city, they bring it on carts, and some of it spills into the road. You know what it's like on market day—the rats and pigeons are everywhere, looking for spilled seed. Usually it rots or gets trodden on, and the ground is hard and stony. But plow it up, make the ground soft, keep people from walking there, and experience tells us some of those old corn seeds will grow. Also, strip all the roofs of their thatch, and you might find old seeds trapped there. Will it do any harm to try these things?" Elise asked them. "Well?"

They had the sense to do as she suggested. They plowed the pathways that led to the lanes, the lanes that led to the roads, and the roads that led to the city. They even dug up the square where the great barn stood, hoping that the wasted seed of past summers would somehow find a way to germinate. And with the spring, the green shoots came—maize and wheat and sometimes even a healthy young shoot from a potato tuber. By the end of summer, the danger of famine was gone.

Elise was brought before the king. He was none other than the young "adviser" whose mustache she had scorned.

"You are due a reward," he said. "It was promised and it shall be given. But first, tell us what made you think of plowing up the roads. Was it your own idea?"

She shook her head.

"Then whose?"

"I hope you'll give me the reward I ask for," said Elise.

"On the honor of a king."

"Then I ask for a life. My father is still alive. He lives in our cellar. It was my father who sent me to tell you to plow up the roads and strip the thatch from the roofs. He has lived for a long time and just knows about these things. What do I understand about seeds? If you ask me, there's a lot of things around here none of us knows about."

No one could deny the justice of that remark, or the wisdom of the man who had saved them. From that time forward, the old people in the kingdom were left to live out their lives in peace.